The Mirror of Human Life

François Couperin: anonymous portrait drawing

Image: Bibliothèque nationale de France, Paris

The Mirror
of Human Life

Reflections on
François Couperin's
Pièces de Clavecin

Jane Clark and
Derek Connon

KEYWORD
PRESS

Published by Keyword Press
291 Sprowston Mews
London E7 9AE
England

First published in 2002 by King's Music
This revised and illustrated edition published
by Keyword Press 2011
Reprinted 2011 and 2015

Designed and typeset by Keyword Press

Printed and bound by Short Run Press Ltd, Exeter, England

ISBN 978-0-9555590-3-7

British Library Cataloguing-in-Publication Data
A catalogue record for this book is available
from the British Library

www.keyword-press.co.uk

CONTENTS

CONTENTS

List of illustrations

School of Politesse

A CD recording has been produced to accompany this book. The programme of the CD, *School of Politesse* (Janiculum JAN D206), played by Jane Clark, attempts to illustrate Couperin's theatrical sense, which develops as his four books of *Pièces de Clavecin* unfold. The first part of the *First Ordre* is relatively conventional, but even here the composer carefully contrasts adjacent pieces, whilst the *Sixth Ordre* reveals his acute sense of characterization. This is followed by the *Thirteenth Ordre*, Couperin's wonderful portrait of human frailty, and in the *Nineteenth Ordre* the precision with which he refers to particular plays is seen. In the final, world-weary *Twenty-Seventh Ordre* Couperin bids his farewell.

School of Politesse is distributed by Janiculum: see
http://www.janiculum.co.uk

Foreword

THE QUOTATION from Jean-François Regnard and Charles Dufresny's play *Les Chinois* was chosen as the title for this book because it describes Couperin's *Pièces de Clavecin* so aptly. Readers must wait until the last *ordre* of all before they find it, by which time they will understand just how appropriate it is. The sub-title is an indication of how the composer's own mind worked in the titles he gave his pieces. Couperin, in his harpsichord music, was clearly entertaining himself and his listeners by writing miniature scenes that are as acutely observed and vividly described as those in the plays he knew so well. Working with a scholar of French literature (who is also a musician) has helped my understanding of the music enormously, particularly the enigmatic final *ordre*. It has made me aware of the vital necessity of being able to see the many layers of meaning in the plays, which in their turn reveal the extent to which Couperin reflected them in his intensely concentrated, and often complicated, pieces.

Not only has Derek Connon widened my vision, he has tidied up my translations, corrected my French, edited the script and provided both Bibliography and Index. It is difficult to acknowledge a task as extensive as this. And the care with which this second edition has been undertaken by the publisher Peter Bavington and the editor Judith Wardman warrants special acknowledgment.

JC

PREFACE

FRANÇOIS COUPERIN (1668–1733) is certainly one of the most important composers of the French baroque. He is perhaps also one of the most enigmatic. Although he is not the only composer of the period to include in his keyboard suites genre pieces with descriptive or evocative titles, no other drew for those titles on such a range of references, many of them coded and satirical. *Les Baricades Mistérieuses* is rightly one of the most famous of his pieces; we may also feel that the title, one of the most impenetrable of all, is almost symbolic, running the risk, like so many of the others, of erecting a mysterious barrier of incomprehension between listener and music. That the appeal of the music remains so strong despite this is partly simply a product of Couperin's greatness, partly a result of the general fact that the meaning of music is of a different order to the meaning of words, so that it speaks to us even if we do not understand the external reference implied by the title. Nevertheless, the communicative power of the music is undoubtedly increased by an understanding of the titles, particularly when so many turn out to indicate an ironic stance or hidden meaning, for, as well as adding an extra-musical dimension, they may also clarify the implications of certain aspects of the music itself. If an understanding of the titles is desirable for the listener, it is surely vital for performers, since it may well have a significant influence on the way a piece should be played.

Perhaps all these titles were transparent for Couperin's contemporaries, perhaps not – it seems likely that some of the more coded references would already have been obscure for anyone outside the composer's immediate circle.

He lived under three régimes: that of Louis XIV, who in the latter part of his reign changed under the influence of his morganatic wife Madame de Maintenon from the great patron of the arts to a figure of religious austerity; the more morally relaxed period of the regency of Philippe d'Orléans; and on into the majority of Louis XV. Couperin had a great interest in the world around him and a lively and wide-ranging taste in literature, principally the theatre. All these things find their way into his music, although people and events are often represented in a coded or a punning way. Clearly it is not enough simply to identify individuals, although even that is not always straightforward; we have to know something about their occupations and personalities in order to be able to decode what the title tells us about the music.

The pieces that bear simple dance titles, which are very much in the minority, clearly pose no problems, but amongst the others, even such a straightforward title as *Le Réveil-matin* (*Fourth Ordre*) may have a story to tell that goes beyond its literal meaning, even if, as the sound of the alarm clock ringing in the music tells us, it can certainly be appreciated on that level too. When we turn to the more obviously obscure titles, however, it can often be impossible to pin down a definitive meaning, and it is likely that there are still some hidden meanings waiting to be discovered. Nevertheless, we are pleased to have discovered in time for this second edition a possible explanation for *La Létiville* (*Sixteenth Ordre*), the only title which had defeated us and previous researchers completely when we published our first edition. Despite those ambiguities which remain, we will feel that we have achieved our goal here if we have advanced research a little towards a better understanding of the full implications of this music.

Couperin's spelling is eccentric, perhaps even by late seventeenth- and early eighteenth-century standards, but original spellings have been retained here for all his titles (including his inconsistent use of accents), lest modernization should obscure a pun or coded reference. Quotations follow the language and spelling of the text or edition consulted. Except where otherwise indicated, translations are by the authors.

In what follows we have built on the work of earlier scholars, but hope also to have brought new insights and revised some old ideas. One of the joys of working on this project has been the dialogue between, on the one hand, a researcher and performer in the field of music and, on the other, a literary critic, each with a lively interest in the other's field, and we hope that this has developed our views in our individual contributions. Jane Clark's analytical catalogue of the individual movements of the *Pièces de Clavecin* is preceded by three essays placing the works and their composer in their more general context, the first, by Jane Clark, on the society in which Couperin moved, and the second, by Derek Connon, on the literary issues raised by the works, and the third, added for this second edition, a study by Jane Clark of the architecture of the *ordres*.

Although this second edition reproduces much of the text of the first edition, we have taken the opportunity to correct a small number of errors, and have significantly expanded a number of entries where we have discovered new evidence or additional information.

DFC

Aspects of the social and cultural background

'Couperin's suites are a sort of refined ballet music. He has re-set the dances played by the orchestra in Lully's operas for harpsichord, and the theatrical twang noticeable in the quaint titles of many of the pieces has stood in the way of a thorough musical development.' That statement, made in 1879 by Edward Dannreuther in the first edition of Grove's *Dictionary*, shows both a profound understanding and a profound *mis*understanding of what Couperin was trying to do. His harpsichord music is indeed a sort of ballet music, but the 'theatrical twang' of the titles has certainly not stood in the way of musical development. Couperin was not constrained by his titles; he was preoccupied with portraying them in musical terms.

Wanda Landowska, though she misinterpreted many of the titles, did recognize their importance. Like so many people she found Couperin a very enigmatic composer. She wrote:

> Couperin's language differs entirely from that of Bach or Handel. In theirs everything is precise, and even when *chiaroscuro* occurs, no misunderstanding can subsist. It has something direct, a nearness that reassures us like a human language, sublime though ritual; it moves in a wholesome way, grips us with its poignancy and appeases us. We return toward life steeled and stronger, able to withstand more easily everyday misery. But what is this elusive anguish that Couperin provokes in us? Whence comes this strange language?[1]

1. *Landowska on Music*, p. 260.

Whence indeed? The only way to find out is to go beyond the face-value of the titles and explore the world behind them.

Couperin said in the preface to *Book I* of his harpsichord pieces: 'I have always had a subject when composing all these pieces: different occasions have provided it. Thus the titles refer to ideas that have occurred to me.' He went on to say that many of the pieces 'are portraits of a kind, which under my fingers have, on occasion, been found to be tolerable likenesses' and that 'their new and diversified character has assured them a favourable reception with the people who matter'. Unlike his chamber music or his church music, most of which was written for the court or the Royal Chapel, much of his harpsichord music must have been written for an informed audience. While no other composer was writing portraits and satires, poets and playwrights were; Couperin joined them in entertaining Parisian society.

The ideas put forward here are not suggested as definitive answers to the problem of solving the meaning of the titles that most of the pieces bear, but they are based on the cumulative picture that emerges when the background to Couperin's 'subjects' is explored. To make that background as vivid as possible, the notes on the pieces in the Catalogue below are, whenever relevant, taken from speeches in the plays that Couperin refers to or contemporary documents. Because the use of the French language has changed so much since the eighteenth century, excerpts from Furetière's *Dictionnaire universel* are included when they illuminate either the titles or the instructions to the player.

For most French composers of the eighteenth century the titles they gave their pieces were a mere convention; for Couperin they were the *raison d'être* of the piece. Unlike his predecessor Lully and his contemporary Rameau, Couperin was not interested in the classical world, the world of the Cyclopes hurling his thunderbolts at the whole universe. Like all educated people at the time he was well aware of classical mythology, but his use of its characters was as a cover for real people with the same characteristics. Couperin was acutely sensitive to human feelings and human foibles, our own feelings and foibles in fact, perennial human conditions, which is what lifts his miniatures on to a universal plane. Lully's and Rameau's heroes and heroines, however tragic, are sufficiently remote for us to be detached from their fates.

In the preface to *Book III* Couperin complains:

> I am always astonished, after the pains I have taken to indicate the appropriate ornaments for my pieces, to hear people who have learnt them without heeding my instructions. Such negligence is unpardonable, the more so as it is no arbitrary matter to put in any ornament one wishes. I therefore declare that my pieces must be performed just as I have marked them, and that they will never make much of an impression on people of real discernment if all that I have indicated is not obeyed to the letter, without adding or taking away anything.

Difficult, and occasionally impossible, though this may be, it is acute attention to all Couperin's minute markings that, ultimately, communicates the composer's intentions. But unless those intentions are understood, the markings often make little sense. Like the Marquise de Lambert, at whose famous salon he played, Couperin was clearly fascinated by psychology.[2] Most of his portraits must be specific, his own reactions to particular people and particular situations, otherwise why would he have claimed that they had been recognized as 'tolerable likenesses' under his fingers? Even the more conventional titles like *Les Vendangeuses* or *Les Moissonneurs*, when the context is considered,

2. Marguerite Glotz and Madeleine Maire, *Salons du XVIIIe siècle*, p. 23.

probably refer to special occasions; they are not simply the conventional topics of his period, despite what is sometimes said.[3] To avoid misunderstanding, it is perhaps worth emphasizing that 'La' at the beginning of a title does not necessarily imply that the subject is feminine; it refers to La Pièce, e.g. the King's piece, the Regent's piece.

Saint Gervais and Saint-Germain-en-Laye

The Pièces de Clavecin are in a sense a musical autobiography. Much about the composer's life that is lacking in documentation is revealed by the titles of the pieces. In 1685 Couperin took up his position as organist of the church of Saint Gervais in Paris, whose congregation included a number of the government officials and their wives portrayed in the Pièces. Saint Gervais is on the edge of the Marais, the district where these wealthy and powerful civil servants built the imposing hôtels at which Couperin played and taught. Contacts he made here led to introductions at the exiled Stuart court at Saint-Germain-en-Laye.[4] It cannot be proved that he was employed there, but the circumstantial evidence is compelling, and it should be considered as part of the background to the harpsichord pieces.[5] Perhaps the strongest argument for Couperin's involvement at the Stuart court is the fact that in 1702

3. Lucinde Braun, 'À la recherche de François Couperin', pp. 43–4. I am grateful to Graham Sadler for drawing my attention to this article.
4. Edward Corp, 'François Couperin and the Stuart court at Saint-Germain-en-Laye, 1691–1712: a new interpretation', and 'The musical manuscripts of "Copiste Z"'.
5. For descriptions of this court see Edward Corp, 'The Jacobite court at Saint-Germain-en-Laye', and 'Les courtisans français à la cour d'Angleterre à Saint-Germain-en-Laye'.

he was made a Chevalier de l'Ordre de Latran by the Pope. Apparently he was the only French composer to receive this honour, and the recommendation must surely have been made by the papal nuncio in France, Cardinal Gualterio, who was very close to the Stuart Queen, Mary of Modena. If, as the website for Chaumes-en-Brie (the ancestral home of the Couperin family) states, this was in recompense for the composer's interest in Italy, it must have been in honour of his early trio sonatas, and possibly other Italian-style music which is lost.[6]

The story of these trios is well-known; they were influenced by Corelli, and the first of them, the composer claimed, was the first of its kind to be written in France. It was called *La Steinquerque*, after a battle won against the English King, William III, considered a usurper by the Stuarts. The victorious troops included James II's Irish regiment. *La Milordine* of the *First Ordre* could be one of the British exiles, who arrived in 1689, and the sombre *Les plaisirs de Saint Germain en Laÿe* could be an ironic reference to the atmosphere created by the intense and somewhat guilt-ridden piety of the deposed King and Queen, James II and Mary of Modena.

Recent work on the Stuart court at Saint-Germain has shown that it was probably here that Couperin heard Italian music for the first time.[7] His *goûts-réunis* style, so prevalent in his chamber music, is particularly noticeable in the *Eighth Ordre*, where the influence of Corelli and his lesser contemporaries like Innocenzo Fede, court composer at Saint-Germain, is felt. The predominant Italian influence at Saint-Germain was due to Mary of Modena.

---

6. <http://www.ville-chaumes-en-brie.fr/Fran_ois%20le%20Grand.html> [accessed December 2009].

7. Edward Corp, 'The exiled court of James II and James III: a centre of Italian music in France, 1689–1712'.

In the *Eighth Ordre* Couperin makes a feature of the angular, declamatory figures of Italian vocal music that were so often parodied by Frenchmen, though never by Couperin, who uses them in his most profound pieces. This he may have learnt from the recitatives in the cantatas of Alessandro Scarlatti and his contemporaries, which were performed at Saint-Germain.

Versailles

From 1694 Couperin was part of the musical establishment at Versailles. As well as his duties as organist at the Royal Chapel for three months of the year, he taught younger members of the royal family. These included the Duc de Bourgogne, Dauphin for one year from 1711 to 1712 and passionate about music, and at least two of the King's illegitimate children, the Dowager Princesse de Conti and the Comte de Toulouse. Couperin taught the Dauphin composition and accompaniment as well as the harpsichord. But it is perhaps a mistake to over-emphasize Couperin's involvement at the court. He was not given any of the official positions that fell vacant, apart from that of part-time organist, a position he shared with Lebègue, Nivers and Buterne, until after the death of Louis XIV. Buterne seems to have been the King's favoured harpsichordist and teacher.[8]

The royal family makes few appearances in the pieces; perhaps portraying its members honestly was too much of a risk. As Derek Connon points out (p. 82), written satire also tended to spare Louis XIV, but not Madame de Maintenon. The King has his magnificent sarabande, *La Majestueuse*, in the *First Ordre*; and Couperin had ample reason to paint Madame de Maintenon as *La*

8. Braun, 'À la recherche de François Couperin', pp. 51–5.

Prude in the *Second Ordre*. It seems that this last, austere 'favourite' (for at the time few people knew of her marriage to the King) makes another appearance in the chaconne, *La Favorite*, in the *Third Ordre*. Taking other aspects of the pieces into account, for one title throws light on another, the most likely candidates for the noble allemande *L'Auguste*, the first piece of all, seem to be the sober and serious Louis-Auguste, Duc Du Maine, the King's favourite and illegitimate son by Madame de Montespan, or the exiled James II, often referred to as Augustus in royalist iconography. In the reign of Louis XV, Couperin portrayed both the King's rejected Spanish fiancée in *La belle Javotte autre fois l'Infante* in the *Twenty-fourth Ordre* and the Polish princess who became his queen as *La Princesse Marie* in the *Twentieth Ordre*.

The Bourbon-Condé family and the Duchesse Du Maine

One of the most important influences on Couperin's *Pièces de Clavecin* was the Bourbon-Condé family. Louis III de Condé (Duc de Bourbon, known as Monsieur le Duc) married Mademoiselle de Nantes, the Duc Du Maine's sister, in 1685, and in 1692 Monsieur le Duc's sister, Anne-Louise-Bénédicte de Bourbon, married the Duc Du Maine. Whether Couperin was employed by Monsieur le Duc before his sister's marriage is not known; it is known, however, that Monsieur le Duc employed him to teach at least two of his children.[9] He also engaged Couperin and his colleagues for concerts to entertain his guests. An important member of the Bourbon-Condé household was La Bruyère, author of the famous *Caractères*, a copy of which

9. Braun, 'À la recherche de François Couperin', p. 41.

Couperin possessed[10]; these literary portraits were clearly a model for Couperin's musical ones. La Bruyère was tutor to both Monsieur le Duc and his sister, the future Duchesse Du Maine. Mademoiselle de Charolais, as she was then, was tremendously influenced by La Bruyère from the age of fifteen.[11] Later, her unconventional life seems to have been a source of constant and often amused inspiration in Couperin's first six *ordres*. She could not bear the court as it was under Madame de Maintenon. 'The Court is becoming so tedious, it is hardly to be endured. The King thinks he is being pious when he arranges for people to be eternally bored.'[12] People complained that it was a monastery in court dress which was becoming duller every day. The Duc Du Maine had been brought up by Madame de Maintenon, in whose eyes he could do no wrong, so the Duchess, given her tastes, must have had more reason than most to escape. This she did, initially to the country chateau of the Du Maines' great friend and the Duke's tutor, the poet Nicolas de Malézieu. He made his chateau of Châtenay a fairyland that filled the Duchess with envy and delight. She suffered from insomnia, so *divertissements*, banquets and fireworks filled the long nights. The elite of the King's Musicians took part beside bands of real peasants who danced and

10. See Michel Antoine, 'Autour de François Couperin', for a list (probably not comprehensive) of Couperin's books included in the posthumous inventory of his possessions. La Bruyère's *Caractères* appears there as *Caractères de Théophraste*. I am grateful to Graham Sadler for this reference.

11. General de Piépape, *A Princess of Strategy*, p. 9.

12. *Letters from Liselotte, Élisabeth Charlotte, Princess Palatine and Duchess of Orléans*, p. 47, 1 October 1687.

sang. The theatre, which was in the gardens, was

> 25 feet square, the wings were closed by interlaced branches. It was roofed with arched festoons of foliage and the floor was magnificently carpeted. It was fronted by a grand portico of greenery with two lesser ones on either side through which one saw the shining light of several huge chandeliers, suspended according to the rules of perspective. In the front was an orchestra pit with tiers on both sides, all covered with greenery like the rest, where one found the elite of the King's musicians, 35 of them directed by Matho.[13]

The theatre occupied the end of a vast marquee where there were more than three hundred guests. This was for the production in 1705 of *La Tarentole*,[14] in which the Duchess played the part of the servant Finemouche. The singers included Marguerite-Louise Couperin, the composer's cousin. Whether Couperin himself was present is not known – the instrumentalists are not recorded – but he appears to refer to this show in *Le Moucheron* (*Sixth Ordre*). There were other *divertissements* at Châtenay in which he could have taken part.

In December 1699 the Duc Du Maine bought the chateau of Sceaux, conveniently next door to Châtenay. This grand property was worthy of his new status as a legitimized son of the King. The couple moved there in 1705. Here invited courtiers and other guests flocked to watch the entertainments, which culminated in the fabulous *Grandes Nuits*. The Duke often escaped to a little tower and occupied himself with geometry and astronomy. He also beautified the gardens. 'I went to look at the Duc Du Maine's new fountains. They are very fine, made of stone to look like pierced rocks, with shell, coral and mother-of-pearl, and rushes

13. Adolphe Jullien, *Les Grandes Nuits de Sceaux, Le Théâtre de la Duchesse Du Maine*, p. 16.

14. A comedy-ballet with text by Nicolas de Malézieu and music by Jean-Baptiste Matho.

with gilded heads.'[15] The *Grandes Nuits*, beginning in 1714, were too late to be the inspiration behind any pieces in Couperin's *Book I*, which was published in 1713, but features of these later events were already there at Châtenay. The *Grandes Nuits* seem to have been in some respects an eighteenth-century equivalent of the seventeenth-century Stuart masques, spectacles designed to draw attention to the court of the Duchesse Du Maine, whilst the full meaning would only be revealed to a few initiates who understood the symbolism. Couperin's name is apparently not mentioned among the musicians who played at these events at Sceaux, but so many of his titles appear to relate to them that it is difficult to feel that this is simply by coincidence.[16] He could, however, have taken part in some of the events at Châtenay or at Clagny, where the Duchess retreated while Sceaux was being made ready for her; he was working for the Duchess's brother at this time, and the two were close. The *divertissements* at Châtenay were accompanied, as we have seen, by 'the elite of the King's musicians'. In July 1702 the King's Musicians took part in a *divertissement* at Châtenay in which, it seems, Couperin might have been involved (see *Les Silvains, First Ordre*). After this was over, Monsieur le Duc invited his sister to visit him at Saint-Maur,[17] and in August 1702 some of the King's Musicians played for him at a concert there, on which occasion Couperin was included (see p. 29). The idea of the 1702 *Fête de Châtenay* seems to have stemmed from Monsieur le Duc, which might strengthen the likelihood of Couperin's involvement.[18] The director of music

---

15. *Letters from Liselotte*, p. 117, 26 October 1704.

16. See Catherine Cessac, 'La duchesse du Maine et la musique'.

17. Piépape, *A Princess of Strategy*, p. 48.

18. See Maurice Barthélemy, 'Chaulieu à Châtenay', pp. 202–4.

for the events at Châtenay was, as we have seen, Jean-Baptiste Matho, who was singing teacher to the Duc de Bourgogne from at least 1699. In April 1700 Couperin began to teach the Duke the harpsichord.[19] Perhaps the appointment was at Matho's suggestion.

The *divertissements* at Châtenay were a novelty – nothing quite like them had happened before – just as Couperin's *Pièces de Clavecin* were 'd'un goût nouveau'.[20] For this reason they must surely form part of the background to his harpsichord music; his immediate colleagues were involved in them even when he himself was not, and musicians never cease to gossip about their latest date. In August 1703 a comedy was staged in which the viol player Forqueray and the flautist Descoteaux (both of whom had played with Couperin at the concerts for Monsieur le Duc) appeared as peasants. This comedy presents various remedies for certain conditions, including *sirop violat* (syrup of violets), which was recognized as a cure, ironically in the circumstances, for insomnia, but which here was deemed excellent for playing the *viole*, the sort of play on words that Couperin enjoyed. It seems that he did not take part on this occasion but he would doubtless have heard about it, possibly with some amusement since Forqueray, who was a proud man, would doubtless have been somewhat indignant.[21]

19. Braun, 'À la recherche de François Couperin', p. 50.
20. Titon Du Tillet, *Le Parnasse françois*, p. 664.
21. Catherine Cessac, 'Un portrait musical de la duchesse du Maine (1676–1753)', Programmes de concert: Versailles, 23 et 28 novembre 2003 (Versailles: Centre de Musique Baroque de Versailles, 2003), <http://philidor.cmbv.fr/jlbweb/jlbWeb?html=cmbv/BurAff&path=/biblio/bur/00/41/41.pdf&ext=pdf> [accessed December 2009], pp. 24–5. This essay gives a fascinating account of events at Châtenay from 1703–1704, pp. 13–30.

Along with pleasures of the spirit went those of the table and the bottle, and the King's Musicians were in attendance throughout. Meals were eaten to the accompaniment of violins, oboes, harpsichords and trumpets. Cantatas in praise of the Duchess were sung at every possible occasion, and if Couperin's lost cantatas ever come to light they will doubtless reveal more about this eccentric lady. The *Fourth Ordre*, with its opening *Marche des Gris-vêtus* (a drinking song), its *Baccanales* and its *Réveil-matin*, very likely refers to Châtenay. At Sceaux the fêtes ended with sumptuous banquets at which drinking songs and amorous verses were sung and an 'irresistible bacchic ardour' overwhelmed the entire company, so there is no reason to suppose that there may not have been similar situations at Châtenay.[22] One of the verses sung by the Duchess ended:

> Du chagrin qui nous possède
> Qui pourra nous délivrer?
> Je n'y vois d'autre remède
> Que celui de s'enivrer.[23]

(From the chagrin that possesses us what can deliver us? I see no other remedy but drink.)

There are many references to the unfortunate musicians having to travel back to Paris in the early hours. After a couple of hours' sleep an alarm would be essential to shake the sleepy harpsichord teacher back into the real world to face his Parisian pupils. The *Third Ordre*, with its theme of darkness, may refer to a *divertissement*; in the first *Grande Nuit*, Night, in a 'lugubrious costume', gave thanks to the Duchess for the preference she

22. Renée Viollier, *Jean-Joseph Mouret le musicien des grâces*, p. 21.
23. Jullien, *Les Grandes Nuits*, p. 10.

accorded her over Day.[24] This theme must already have been present at Châtenay, even if only in the complaints of the weary musicians. At the same time it may equally well refer to the sombre atmosphere that had invaded the court under the influence of Madame de Maintenon.

The Duchesse Du Maine, influenced by La Bruyère, prided herself on Sceaux being an up-dated version of the seventeenth-century salons, and this aspect of life there is reflected in the *Sixth Ordre*. The original blue-stockings, on whom the Duchess modelled herself, instituted the custom of drawing literary portraits, a custom La Bruyère revived in his *Caractères* and one that thrived once more under the Duchess, initially at Châtenay. Whilst the literary portrait faded out again, Couperin's revolutionary musical *caractères* dealt a death blow to the conventional dance suite in France and started a flood of character pieces with titles. Very few of these *nouvelle vague* harpsichord pieces have anything like Couperin's theatrical sense, and very few attempt to portray their titles as Couperin did.[25] But to be fair to the Duchesse Du Maine, if Couperin presents the public, theatrical side of this formidably intelligent woman, her intimates saw another. Mademoiselle de Launay felt that: 'no one ever discoursed with more discernment, with greater nicety and vivacity, nor in a manner more noble and unaffected.'[26] She also inspired loyal friendship. The Marquise de Lambert was, according to Mademoiselle de Launay, 'infinitely devoted to her interests'. The

24. Madame de Staal de Launay, *Memoirs*, I, p. 18.

25. For a general picture of the use of titles and how Couperin fitted into it, see David Fuller, 'Of portraits, "Sapho" and Couperin: titles and characters in French instrumental music of the High Baroque' and 'Portraits and characters in instrumental music of seventeenth- and eighteenth-century France'.

26. Madame de Staal de Launay, *Memoirs*, I, p. 135.

Marquise had got wind of the impending arrest of the Duchess for her plotting against the Regent after the death of Louis XIV, and at great risk sent a servant to warn her.[27]

Court and aristocracy

Couperin took part in concerts held at the chateaux of the royal family and the aristocracy. He played for the King at Versailles: 'Sunday 23 November 1701. After supper the King heard an exquisite concert of Italian airs in his private apartments, executed by Messrs Forcroy[28] on the viol, Couperin on the harpsichord, and the young Baptiste (Anet II) on the violin.'[29] In August 1702, as we saw, a concert took place at Saint-Maur, where the Dauphin was staying as a guest of Monsieur le Duc. After a day's hunting wolves in the forest of Sénart, the Princesse de Conti arrived for supper, which was served at seven o'clock; then there was music, performed by the gentlemen Cocherot and Thévenard of the Opéra and the ladies Couperin and Maupin. Couperin accompanied on the spinet. Messrs Visée, Forqueray, Philbert, Descoteaux and several violins were also part of the concert. This was on Monday. 'On Tuesday Mlles. Couperin and Maupin sang a motet at the Dauphin's Mass, accompanied by Monsieur Couperin on the spinet.' That night, while they were playing cards after supper, 'Mlle. Couperin sang some recitatives from the old operas, accompanied by Messrs Couperin and Forqueray'.[30]

27. Madame de Staal de Launay, *Memoirs*, I, p. 207.

28. A contemporary variant spelling of Forqueray (see below). It is the latter that is now usually adopted.

29. *Mercure Galant*, quoted in Philippe Beaussant, *François Couperin*, p. 77.

30. *Mercure Galant*, in Beaussant, *François Couperin*, p. 77.

Couperin, with 'Messrs Visée, Forcroy, Rebel, Favre, Philbert and Descoteaux' had played at Monsieur le Duc's chateau of Saint-Maur in July 1701.[31]

This gives an idea of how closely Couperin's life was involved with the Bourbon-Condé family and how much time he must have spent on their country estates. Aware of all that went on, he had a perpetual store of subjects for his pieces. Monsieur le Duc was keen to be as close to the royal family as possible and he frequently entertained the Dauphin. The father of Couperin's musical pupil, *Monseigneur*, as he was called, was consumed by a passion for hunting, but after the hunt the company relaxed to the sounds of the best musicians in the land. Saint-Maur was a charming chateau very near Paris, on the banks of the Marne, with a garden designed by Le Nôtre. Monsieur le Duc was particularly fond of it and his sister nicknamed him the Baron de Saint-Maur. The company moved from *divertissements* at Châtenay or Sceaux to hunting parties and concerts at Saint-Maur and the elite of the King's Musicians followed.

Philippe d'Orléans and the Prince de Conti

The King's nephew, Philippe d'Orléans, became Regent of France on Louis XIV's death in 1715. He makes his first appearance in the *Pièces* in *La Coribante* in the *Twelfth Ordre* and he is the subject of the whole of the *Thirteenth Ordre*, one of the most compassionate portraits of human frailty ever created. His interest in the arts and

31. *Mercure Galant*, in Beaussant, *François Couperin*, p. 78.

Philippe II, Duc d'Orléans, Regent of France 1715–1723:
engraving by Claude Duflos

Image: Bibliothèque nationale de France

sciences is referred to in the sad and somewhat learned allemande, *La Régente ou La Minerve*, that opens the *Fifteenth Ordre*, which continues to refer to the Regent. The *Sixteenth Ordre* opens with a portrait of François-Louis de Bourbon, Prince de Conti. Both these highly talented and capable men were denied positions and responsibility by Louis XIV, who feared them as rivals to his own sons, particularly the Duc Du Maine. The King also had a not unreasonable fear of subversive influences among the Princes of the Blood and the aristocracy. Couperin, however, clearly felt great sympathy with these two men, who turned to debauchery to relieve their boredom. Élisabeth-Charlotte, Duchesse d'Orléans, writes of her son:

> My son enjoys neither hunting, shooting nor gambling but loves all the arts, especially painting. The painters say his judgement is very good. He loves chemistry, he loves conversation and talks well. He has studied hard and knows a lot because his memory is good. He loves music and he loves women. I often wish there were a little less of the latter because it takes him into such bad company and makes him ruin himself.[32]

The Duchess despaired because her husband, the King's unpleasant brother, refused to speak to him about his dissolute life and she sadly says: 'Had he been brought up to something better and more worthwhile he would be quite a different person.'[33] Many people shared this feeling, even the critical Saint Simon, who was a loyal and despairing friend. The Regent possessed a quality that would endear him to any musician: 'He never put on airs or paraded superior knowledge, but spoke to each man as to

32. *Letters from Liselotte*, p. 133, 7 February 1709.
33. *Letters from Liselotte*, p. 82, 2 February 1698.

an equal.'[34] His mother said that 'he would rather mix with common painters and musicians than with the right people'.[35]

It was partly the influence of François-Louis, Prince de Conti, that led Philippe d'Orléans along the road to ruin. The lives of these two brilliant men are a sad reflection on absolute monarchy. Saint Simon is sympathetic to this victim too:

> He took pains to please everyone, cobblers, lackeys, chair-porters, ministers of State, lords and generals alike, and his friendliness was so easy he succeeded with them all. Thus he was a constant joy in Society and at the Court, the idol of the army and the masses, the hero of young officers, and the hope of scholars and men of science. He had an extremely good brain, enlightened, precise and well informed.

Saint Simon also adds the revealing remark: 'He kept a cool head amidst all the futility of the Court.'[36] It is likely Couperin felt this futility too.

Singers and actresses

Couperin also found the mistresses of his patrons, his own colleagues in fact, an endless source of inspiration. The singers and actresses who had such a dubious reputation feature in many of the pieces, also in his two surviving vocal canons, 'Woman between two Sheets' and 'The three Vestal Virgins and the three Lechers'. The words of these show that to put Couperin in a rarefied atmosphere is a grave mistake. There is no reason to

---

34. *Historical Memoirs of the Duc de Saint Simon*, II, p. 428.
35. *Letters from Liselotte*, p. 88, 26 July 1699.
36. *Saint Simon*, I, p. 420.

suppose that many of his harpsichord pieces are not as explicitly sexy as these verses.

La Femme entre deux Draps

La femme entre deux draps
Gravement fait le cas.
Les Jeannetons et les Fanchons
Ne vont pas que par sauts et par bonds,
Mais La Catin va si grand train,
Que qui ne la tiendroit au crin
Seroit désarçonné, démonté, culbuté, soudain.

(Woman between two sheets goes seriously wild. With your Jeannetons and Fanchons you get a rough ride, but a Catin goes at it so fast that anyone who didn't hang on to her mane would be suddenly unsaddled, thrown and somersaulted.)

Les Trois Vestales Champêtres et Les Trois Poliçons

Quel bruit soudain vient troubler nos retraites?
Que cherchés vous? fuyés, téméraires mortels,
Pour d'autres que pour nous elles ne sont pas faites;
Fuyés, fuyés, téméraires mortels,
Fuyés, Profanes, respectes nos Dieux et nos autels.
Louison, Suzon, Thérése,
Dans un fiâcre à notre aise
Nous venons pour vous voir.
De nous bien recevoir,
Tel est vôtre devoir:
Faites donc bien les choses,
Nous aimons bouches closes,
Et pour payer vos frais
Voicy trois bilboquets.[37]

(What noise suddenly disturbs our solitude? What are you seeking? Flee, rash mortals, this place is meant only for us; flee, flee, rash

37. The game of *bilboquet* involves catching either a ball in a cup or a ball with a hole on a spike. The potentially obscene appearance of these toys means that the implication here is erotic.

mortals, flee, non-believers, respect our gods and our altars. Louison, Suzon, Thérése, comfortable in our carriage we are coming to see you. It is your duty to give us a good welcome: so do things nicely, we love mouths closed, and to pay your fees here are three toys.)

These poems are typical of the satirical verses of the time. Whilst Lully, a court composer, was so often portrayed in the most scurrilous of these, Couperin, also a court composer, wrote them himself in his harpsichord pieces. The royal family is not spared by the satirists, but Couperin, apart from veiled digs at Madame de Maintenon, is tactful with the members he had to take care with and sympathetic to those whose lives were ruined by the establishment.

The harpsichord piece entitled *Les Vestales* (*Sixteenth Ordre*) was one of those that was parodied, that is had words added by popular poets.[38] In spite of his irony Couperin reveals, in the preface to *Book III*, that he was rather flattered by these parodies:

> I would never have imagined that my pieces should attain immortality, but since several famous poets have honoured them with a parody, this distinction might very well, in time to come, endow them with a reputation originally due entirely to the charming parodies they have inspired. In this new volume, therefore, I am expressing in advance to my obliging associates, all the gratitude that such flattering company inspires in me, by providing them, in this third book, with abundant scope for exercising their Minerva.

Stories about the affairs of singers and actresses abound. One example concerning 'Fanchon' and 'Louison' shows how these

38. See Davitt Moroney, 'The parodies of François Couperin's harpsichord pieces'.

were conducted. The Dauphin took a fancy to Françoise Moreau (known as Fanchon), 'pretty courtesan of the opera'. He asked Lully's son-in-law Dumont, who arranged these things, to write to her on his behalf. Unfortunately the letter arrived in the hands of her sister Louison (Louise Moreau), 'who was very ugly', but who presented herself promptly at the chateau of Meudon. The Dauphin received her 'and made the best of it'. However, Dumont, discovering the mistake, arrived with Fanchon 'and knocked on the door. "You are mistaken, Monseigneur" he cried. [...] No reply. Dumont redoubled his efforts and at last Monseigneur opened the door and protested that he was quite content with Louison and that he would see her sister another time'. He gave Dumont ten *louis* by way of consolation for Fanchon, who was so angry at being sent away without being seen that 'she threw the money back in Dumont's face'.[39]

A Dutchman warned foreign travellers:

> They should guard against too close acquaintance with girls from the opera or the comedy. Almost all those who are at all beautiful are supported by illustrious and rich noblemen. [...] I knew several of my compatriots who thought they could touch the stars with their fingers when they succeeded in contracting an amorous relationship with one of them. [...] You find, apart from the comedy and the opera, plenty of other charming and pretty ladies, but an affair with an actress seems more alluring. People forget that the latter have only the prestige of the stage, and that seen elsewhere they lose half their beauty. This consists above all in the rouge and the powder in which they are covered. They resemble apples of Paradise; their appearance is of incomparable beauty, they look charming, but when you touch them they fall to dust. It costs a lot to feed horses like these. It is necessary to have a well-lined purse to carry one off when you are in

39. Bois-Jourdain, *Mélanges*, I, p. 35.

competition with rich French noblemen, for these ladies are hard to please.[40]

Children of these liaisons were often brought up by their royal or aristocratic fathers. The Duchesse d'Orléans wrote of one of her son's daughters:

> I went to the theatre, where Baron and the Desmares were acting. The Desmares has a daughter by my son. He has not legitimized her but he is very fond of her. He married her off to a man of quality, the Marquis de Ségur, who used to be a page to the late King. When this lady is in our box the Desmares can't stop gazing at her, and one often sees tears in her eyes.[41]

Of his three illegitimate children Philippe d'Orléans legitimized only one, a son by one of his mother's ladies in waiting, the Comtesse d'Argenton. 'The other one', the Duchess wrote, 'now a lad of eighteen, is an abbot, for my son doesn't want to have his bastards whom he hasn't recognized founding families. He was the son of La Florence. She was a beautiful girl, a dancer at the Opéra; she is dead now.'[42] This was Florence Pellegrin (see *La Florentine, Second Ordre*). Rigaud painted a fine portrait of their son, Charles de Saint Albin, who became Archbishop of Cambrai.

The Dauphin had a daughter by the celebrated actress La Raisin. She was brought up by the Dowager Princesse de Conti, who was very close to the Dauphin. Marie-Anne, Dowager Princesse de Conti, was the daughter of Louis XIV and Louise de

---

40. J. C. Nemeitz, *Séjour de Paris*, in Alfred Franklin, *La Vie privée d'autrefois*, XXI, *La Vie de Paris sous la Régence*, p. 45.
41. *Letters from Liselotte*, p. 225, 4 July 1720.
42. *Letters from Liselotte*, p. 184, 16 July 1716.

La Vallière and a pupil of Couperin.[43] 'Monsieur le Dauphin [...]
spends his entire time at the Princesse de Conti's. For all his
laughing at her, he is ruled by her as surely as his father is ruled by
Mme. de Maintenon. He is in love with an actress.'[44] Their
daughter was in despair when her father died (see *La Fleurie ou La
tendre Nanette*, First *Ordre*). La Raisin was Françoise Pitel de
Longchamp, known as Fanchon Longchamps (see *La Tendre
Fanchon*, Fifth *Ordre*). She married the actor Jean-Baptiste Raisin,
who died in 1693.

Satire

Couperin's sense of humour should not be underestimated:
Molière was not the only person to ridicule anything he thought
precious. Painting was a popular topic at the eighteenth-century
salons. Discussions were often thought pretentious by the artists
themselves. Charles Coypel parodied the language:

> Mais, mais, Monsieur, le caractère! Le caractère, Monsieur, le
> caractère! Voyez comme ces sourcils sont frappés, ce front heurté et
> peint à pleine couleur, puis retouché à gras, pouf, pouf, pouf!
> Comme ces gens-là faisaient rouler leur pinceau! Comme cela est
> fouetté! Ah! Monsieur, cela est divin![45]

> (But, but, sir, the character! The character, Monsieur, the character!
> See how the eyebrows are astonished, the furrowed brow painted
> with a full brush, then thickly retouched, plop, plop, plop! How
> these people make their brushes roll! It's as though it's whipped! Ah!
> Sir! It's divine.)

43. Titon Du Tillet, *Le Parnasse françois*, p. 664.
44. *Letters from Liselotte*, p. 77, 18 January 1697.
45. Glotz and Maire, *Salons*, p. 35.

Coypel's highly successful illustrations for *Don Quixote* were painted as cartoons for tapestries, and engraved and published in 1724. Couperin possessed sixteen engravings of illustrations for *Don Quixote*.[46] He seems to be similarly mocking the *littérateurs* in *Les Laurentines* (*Third Ordre*). One of his vocal canons, *Les Agioteurs au désespoir* (*The Speculators in Despair*), sheds crocodile tears for victims of John Law's disastrous financial schemes:

> Pleurez, pleurez mes tristes yeux,
> Fortune hélas! Tu me flattois:
> Mais, pour me mieux trahir
> Faut-il rentrer dans le néant de mes aveux;
> Quel sort fatal! Ah, quel supplice;
> Oh Dieux! Trop justes Dieux!
> Que mes accents et que mes plaintes
> Pénètrent jusqu'aux Cieux![47]

(Weep, weep, my sad eyes! Fortune alas! You flattered me: but, to add insult to injury, must I go back to surviving on empty promises; What bad luck! Ah, what torment; oh Gods! Too just Gods! May my expressions and my lamentations reach the Heavens!)

In *Héraclite, Démocrite, Diogène* he mocks philosophers:

HÉRACLITE:
> Pleurez, pleurez mes tristes yeux,
> Ici-bas tout m'est odieux.

DÉMOCRITE:
> Avec du tabac, du vin, du jeu,
> Quelque Chloris

46. Antoine, 'Autour de François Couperin', p. 119.
47. Greer Garden, 'Un canon à cinq inédit de Couperin', *Bulletin de l'Atelier d'Études sur la Musique Française des XVIIe & XVIIIe Siècles*, 10 (2001–2002), pp. 16–17. I am grateful to Graham Sadler for drawing my attention to this.

> Et bon acceuil chez mes amis,
> J'incague les tristes ennuis.

DIOGÈNE:
> Pour moi, je vois tranquillement
> Rire et pleurer également.[48]

(HERACLITUS: Weep, weep, my sad eyes, Everything in this life is hateful to me. DEMOCRITUS: With some baccy, some wine, some gambling, A wench like Chloris and a warm welcome among my friends, I scorn sad cares. DIOGENES: As for me, I regard with indifference both laughter and tears.)

Playing with words, something Couperin does with names (see for instance *La Logiviére, Fifth Ordre*, and *La Létiville, Sixteenth Ordre*), was quite common. A vivid example is the signboard of a wine merchant, *Vin sans Eau* ('Wine without Water'), depicted as 20, 100, 0 (vingt = 20, cent = 100 and 0, pronounced as the letter O). 'Many signs were creative mutilators, or multipliers, of language, drawing upon visual/verbal puns for their effect.'[49]

Comments on, and by, Couperin's colleagues are an invaluable aid towards understanding his harpsichord music. He said himself, in the preface to *Book I*, that he would rather be moved than astonished. Montéclair, in the preface to his *Brunètes anciènes et modernes*, said:

> Je suis persuadé que Messieurs Marais et Couperin, qui par la beauté de leurs ouvrages, se sont attiré l'estime universelle, conviendront que les petits Airs tendres qu'ils ont meslé parmi leurs autres pieces, sont les plus difficilles à executer par le sentiment qu'ils demandent et qu'ils ne les affectent pas moins que leur grandes pièces.

48. See Graham Sadler, 'A philosophy lesson with François Couperin?' (Sadler's translation).
49. Julie Anne Plax, *Watteau and the Cultural Politics of Eighteenth-Century France*, p. 164.

(I am persuaded that Messieurs Marais and Couperin, who, by the beauty of their works, have attracted universal esteem, would agree that the little tender airs they have mixed amongst their other pieces, are the most difficult to execute because of the feeling they demand and that they move them no less than their grand pieces.)

At the other end of the scale, the dramatic, declamatory moments should not be overlooked. The bass, Gabriel-Vincent Thévenard (see *La Gabriéle, Tenth Ordre*), with whom Couperin worked, was famous for the declamation that was the practice of the old actors.[50] *Les Rozeaux* (*The Reeds, Thirteenth Ordre*) must be one of the most deeply touching portrayals of human frailty ever written, a far cry from the boldly dramatic allemandes, *La Raphaéle* (*Eighth Ordre*) or *La Verneüil* (*Eighteenth Ordre*), which is, in fact, a portrait of one of the old actors.

Watteau

Much has been made of the similarity between Couperin and Watteau but it is possible to take the idea too far. There is one basic difference, and that is that Watteau, as most people observe, was an onlooker who described his world from a distance, whereas Couperin was very much a part of it. Perhaps because of the perfection of his craft, and because of the association in everyone's minds with the painter, Couperin has been placed in the same idealized world, which has led to a basic misunderstanding of his portraits. His acute sense of the ridiculous and his clearly intimate knowledge of the dubious morals of his theatrical friends, which he evidently relished describing, are swept under a polite carpet of tasteful ornaments.

50. Émile Campardon, *L'Académie Royale au XVIIIᵉ siècle*, II, p. 307.

One demonstrable connection between Watteau, Couperin and Rameau is the common use of some titles. Since the titles to Watteau's paintings were added after his death by the engraver, Jean de Julienne, these were probably taken from the musical portraits. It seems that painters often turned to musical subjects for inspiration, rather than the other way about, so it is perfectly possible that Watteau was indeed painting what Rameau or Couperin described in musical terms.[51] Some titles, 'Indiscretion' for instance, belonged to a common fund portrayed by painters and composers alike and not only in France. One of Watteau's paintings is named *La Villageoise* and Rameau wrote a piece called *La Villageoise*, said to be based on a folk tune. In the painting a peasant girl stands in a stream; the harpsichord piece breaks from its folk-like tune into the typical musical portrayal of running water. In Watteau's painting *L'Enchanteur* a young man plays the guitar to two girls on the banks of a river. In Couperin's *L'Enchanteresse* (feminine because of *la pièce*; *First Ordre*), which is written in the lute/guitar register, again, the music breaks into what could be a portrayal of running water. There is a Watteau painting called *L'Indiscret* in which a girl, in a very seductive pose, sits on the grass holding a spindle, while a boy plays the flute at her feet. Both spinning and the flute had erotic connotations. In Rameau's *L'Indiscrète* from his *Pièces de Clavecin en Concert* the harpsichord part is the classic musical spinning wheel, still used in the nineteenth century, while the flute makes amorous advances. Watteau also painted *La Fileuse* (*The Spinner*), and one of Couperin's portraits is *La Fileuse* (*Twelfth Ordre*). Paris being so small and their having so many acquaintances in common strongly suggests that these three men knew each other. When Rameau was organist at the Jesuit church in the Rue Saint Jacques

51. I am grateful to Jo Headley for this observation.

from 1706 to 1709, Watteau was working in the print shops in that street. Rameau left Paris in 1709 and Watteau died in 1721, but when the composer returned to the city the following year he immediately entered the circle of friends to which Watteau had belonged.

Like Watteau, Couperin drew many portraits from the theatre; but their outlooks are very different. Couperin was sixteen years older than Watteau, and thirty-four when Watteau arrived in Paris in 1702. He was twenty-nine when Evaristo Gherardi's company of Italian comedians was disbanded in 1697. His experience of this troupe was real. His references to it in *Book IV* are retrospective and nostalgic, but precise. Watteau's painting of *Le Départ des Comédiens Italiens en 1697*, painted some time between 1703 and 1709, can be read as a political allegory.[52] The figures in his *fêtes galantes* represent aristocrats, bankers and other members of Parisian society who attended these, dressed in costumes of the comedians. His paintings do not portray the actual theatre.

The theatre

Theatrical life in Paris when Couperin was a young man centred on the Théâtre de Bourgogne, where the King's Comédiens Français and the King's Comédiens Italiens played on alternate nights. Apart from minor squabbles all went reasonably smoothly until 1696, when the Italians overstepped the mark with obscene jokes and innuendos about the King and Madame de Maintenon. Louis XIV warned them, but his warning went unheeded. As

52. Julie Anne Plax, *Watteau and the Cultural Politics of Eighteenth-Century France*, pp. 7–52.

Derek Connon explains (pp. 71–3), the King's true reason for disbanding the troupe remains unclear, but it seems likely that the prudery of Madame de Maintenon had something to do with it:

> Sermon and Mass may have their point so far as the next world is concerned, but for this one they are bitterly dreary. If by experiencing little joy and great tribulation one earns the right to go to heaven, my earnings should be enough to make me a great saint. If the rumours are to be believed, our tedium will become greater still, because we hear that all the operas and plays are to be abolished. The Sorbonne has instructions to take the matter in hand. What seems so astonishing to me is that they concentrate on such innocent things while all the vices are in full swing. No-one says a single word against poisoning, violence, and that horrible sodomy; all the clergy preach against the poor theatre, which does nobody any harm, and where vice is punished and virtue rewarded. It makes me furious.[53]

A week later the Duchesse d'Orléans was able to write with relief: 'Thank God the theatre is to stay. This greatly annoys the great old man's hag, as she was responsible for the proposed ban.'[54] Madame de Maintenon was 'greatly disliked' in Paris. 'Whenever she went there the people called out threats after her. In the end she didn't dare drive about in her own coach.'[55] Couperin clearly loved the Italian troupe and its plays, so this may well strengthen the argument that Madame de Maintenon appears as *La Prude*. Members of the disbanded company were at once welcomed by the Duchesse Du Maine, who used to act in comedies with them, by the Prince de Conti and Philippe d'Orléans, all the members of the royal family who took a delight in needling Louis XIV and all the people that Couperin evidently

53. *Letters from Liselotte*, p. 68, 16 December 1694.
54. *Letters from Liselotte*, p. 68, 23 December 1694.
55. *Letters from Liselotte*, p. 226, 6 August 1720.

found congenial. The Italian actors also took refuge in the theatres at the great Parisian Fairs of Saint-Laurent and Saint-Germain. Forbidden to use words, they mimed their actions and displayed the vital directions on billboards.

The plays were preceded at the Fairs by rope-dancers, to whom Couperin refers in *Le Tic-Toc-Choc ou les Maillotins* (*Eighteenth Ordre*), the Maillot family being celebrated rope-dancers. A Dutch traveller describes the Fair theatre:

> The greatest entertainments of the Foire Saint Germain are given by troupes of rope-dancers. There are sometimes four or five of these troupes who set up their theatre partly inside the fairground and partly outside. Everyone comes there. Moreover at this time of year (3 February until two weeks after Easter) there are many spectators, even spectators of quality, since these people have left their country houses, also a number of officers have returned from the army (in times of war) not to speak of all the provincials who are in Paris for trials or other reasons. I have often noticed that not only the opera and the comedy but also five troupes of rope-dancers have been besieged to the point where they have to turn people away. The troupe that at any one time takes the lead is the most frequented, people fall on their tent as though they were going to take it by storm. Rope-dancing is less studied than the comedy they play afterwards. This is because there are in these troupes some actors from the so-called Théâtre Italien, closed a long time ago by order of the court. At the fair things are allowed that at other times would be forbidden; in this way the actors, under pretext of rope-dancing, have resuscitated their original theatre, only it is, they say, but a shadow of the other. At the beginning, not having permission to speak or to sing they confined themselves to presenting their plays with signs and acrobatics but before long they sang them. For this liberty they paid an annual sum to the opera. The plays they present are for the most part taken from the *Théâtre italien* of Evaristo Gherardi and according to the success that they have, the troupes sometimes play the same play for a fortnight. The troupes are very jealous of one another and move Heaven and earth to attract the greatest number of spectators. Nevertheless the one with the best

Harlequin usually scores over the others; the low and burlesque words and the impudent gestures do not diminish the success of a play. I have often seen, to my astonishment, ladies of quality hearing and seeing these obscenities without blushing: moreover, they cannot hide the satisfaction they derive from the spectacle since they laugh with all their hearts. But, why worry? C'est la mode de Paris. The more earthy and grotesque a joke is, the more it amuses. All is permitted to Harlequin and Columbine, the two good children.

There was a danger of losing life and limb at the Fairs from the quarrels that broke out and the pickpockets. There were stalls, monsters, men posing as wild beasts, puppets and acting animals. 'If you can avoid circulating with women and girls,' counsels the Dutchman, 'so much the better. They are very embarrassing and you don't escape unscathed.' However, if you did have the misfortune to get caught up you just had to be in a good humour and go along with whatever pleased them. 'The obscene postures of the girls who dance shock reason and modesty, and as for the rope-dancers themselves, the feats they perform, sometimes at peril of their lives, make the spectators' hair stand on end.'[56]

Quite how Couperin became involved in the theatre is not clear, but there is one possibility. Couperin's mother's maiden name was Guérin. Molière's widow, Armande Béjart, married the actor Isaac-François Guérin in 1677. They had a son, Nicolas-Armand-Martial Guérin, who inherited Molière's manuscripts. He arranged a *Pastorale Heroïque*, *Mirtil et Mélicerte*, based on fragments of Molière, which was presented at Fontainebleau in October 1698, with music by Lalande. It was staged again in January and February 1699 at the Comédie Française; the fourteen musical interludes on this occasion were different. The Parfaict brothers, in their *Histoire du Théâtre-Français*, quote the satirical

56. Nemeitz, *Séjour de Paris*, in Franklin, *La Vie privée d'autrefois*, XXI, pp. 101 ff.

poet François Gacon as attributing them to Lalande but also relate that Nicolas Grandval assured them that they were composed by Couperin 'si célèbre par ses belles Pièces de Clavecin'. Grandval played the harpsichord in court entertainments at the time, so perhaps he was in the better position to know.[57] It has to be admitted that the music of these interludes does not bear any particular Couperin-like characteristics, but perhaps he was trying to keep a low profile in the face of Lalande's recent contributions. But if Grandval was correct in his attribution it raises interesting questions as to Couperin's mother's family and connections that could have led her son to the theatre.[58]

Another possible connection is the actress Françoise Pitel de Longchamp (see p. 37 and *La Tendre Fanchon, Fifth Ordre*). She persuaded the Dauphin to order the Comédie Française, which at first rejected it, to present the play, with the new interludes.[59]

Evaristo Gherardi

Though Couperin makes many references to the Comédiens Français, perhaps his greatest sympathy of all was for the King's Comédiens Italiens. The director of this troupe, and its Arlequin, was Evaristo Gherardi. A highly cultured man, he was born in Prato, but brought up and educated at a Jesuit school in Paris. A contemporary of Couperin, he died in 1700 as the result of a fall

57. Lionel Sawkins, *A Thematic Catalogue of the Works of Michel-Richard de Lalande*, p. 519.

58. I am very grateful to Graham Sadler for obtaining photocopies of these Interludes for me from the Bibliothèque Nationale.

59. Sawkins, *A Thematic Catalogue of the Works of Michel-Richard de Lalande*, p. 519.

at the chateau of Saint-Maur, where he had been presenting one of his plays.[60] The Duchesse d'Orléans, the Regent's mother, a keen theatregoer and an astute critic, was the dedicatee of Gherardi's *Le Théâtre italien*, a collection of plays by French authors, in French, based on old *commedia dell'arte* plots, with gaps left for improvisation in the old *commedia* style. As Derek Connon points out (pp. 62–5) with regard to Regnard and Dufresny's *Les Chinois*, many of the plays contain a complicated mixture of French and Italian elements, which may well have been one of the attractions for Couperin considering his interest in *les goûts réunis*. Regnard and Dufresny wrote the best of them, working separately at first but eventually as a team.

The stage directions of these plays call for an immense amount of music of all kinds, sometimes for quite large forces. A lot of the songs survive; most of them are anonymous, and Couperin's name is not among those that do appear. However, several of the songs have a characteristic which is also true of Couperin, the use of the minor third of the dominant when a modulation is being made to the dominant key.[61] Couperin does this in his *brunette*, *Zéphyre modère en ces lieux*. This form of modulation, or melodic twist, occurs in some of the harpsichord pieces as well, a well-known example being bar 7 of *Le Rossignol-en-amour* in the *Fourteenth Ordre*. If this is indeed a characteristic of Couperin, it might indicate that he wrote some of the music for Gherardi's troupe; and certainly some of the surviving tunes do have a distinctly Couperin-like flavour. He would perhaps not have wanted his name attached to them because he depended on Louis

60. Émile Campardon, *Les Comédiens du Roi de la Troupe Italienne*, I, p. 239.

61. Donald Jay Grout, 'The Music of the Italian Theatre at Paris, 1682–97', p. 167.

XIV for part of his livelihood, and by the time Gherardi published the music the troupe had been officially expelled by the King. Couperin would in any case have worked closely with actors from the Italian troupe when playing for those members of the royal family who patronized its members both before and after it had been disbanded. The Marquis de Dangeau reports in his diary on 26 November 1694, that is before the theatre was closed, that the Dauphin was entertained at Le Petit Luxembourg by 'Descoteaux, Filbert and Visée for music, Mezzetin and Pasquariel for some Italian scenes'. These performers, with whom Couperin so often played and who had once more been summoned by Monsieur le Duc, were not joined by Couperin on this occasion, but there must have been many other such entertainments in which he was included.

Jean-François Regnard

The lives of Regnard and Dufresny, even when stripped of the legends that originated with the authors themselves, are as colourful as their plays. Couperin possessed five volumes of Regnard's works, and he must have known both men well.[62] Jean-François Regnard was thirteen years older than Couperin, the son of a well-to-do merchant. He served his apprenticeship and then embarked on his first adventure. He travelled to Italy and was then captured by pirates and sold as a slave in Algeria. Discovering a talent for making bird cages, he was let off the most unpleasant tasks, but on being recaptured after a failed attempt to escape he had a hard time. Eventually a ransom of 2,000 *livres* was paid and

62. Antoine, 'Autour de François Couperin', p. 122, where they appear as 'Œuvres de Renard'.

Jean-François Regnard: engraving by
P. A. Tardieu after Hyacinthe Rigaud,
from *Œuvres Complets de Regnard*, 1810

he was free. He worked in Paris for a while and then set out again, for reasons which are not clear, on an extraordinary voyage, this time northwards. He travelled through Belgium and Holland to Copenhagen and Stockholm, kissing the hands of both kings. He then went to Lapland, where he went down copper mines and was appalled at the conditions endured by the miners. Travelling south again, he went down silver mines, stopped off at the library at Uppsala, visited the astronomer Hevelius in Danzig and was shown his famous map of the moon, his telescope and his books. He dined at the table of the Polish King and Queen, the Queen being Maria Casimira, later Domenico Scarlatti's patron in Rome. Despite his warm welcome in Poland, Regnard scoffed at the arrogance of the nobles and still more at their excessive piety; their devotion seemed to him more show than real, and he felt that a Pole would think it a good action if he were to kill a man for eating meat on Fridays. Couperin mocked these Polish nobles in his *Air dans le goût Polonois* in *La Princesse Marie* (*Twentieth Ordre*).

On his return to Paris Regnard purchased an office of Conseiller Trésorier de France, an undemanding position. Racine and La Bruyère had held similar posts. He also bought the chateau of Grillon, an idyllic spot on the banks of the river Orge, between Paris and Chartres. Here he and his friends hunted wild boar, gambled, and drank, founding an abbey consecrated to Bacchus. The library included twenty books of music, and there was a harpsichord and a bass viol. Among his friends Regnard counted the Loyson (Loison) sisters, Jeanne and Catherine, known as Doguine and Tontine, one being a blonde and the other a brunette. These sisters must surely figure among Couperin's portraits, possibly more than once, and an obvious candidate is *Les Juméles* of the *Twelfth Ordre*, others being *Les Nonètes, First Ordre*, and *Les Chérubins ou L'aimable Lazure, Twentieth Ordre*. They were not twins, in fact, but seem to have been inseparable. Fontenelle, the celebrated French author and philosopher, was one victim of the charm of 'Quatre beaux yeux'. At their house in Paris the most illustrious youth and the elite of the court congregated. The glittering company gambled, danced, ate sumptuous meals and listened to music. The sisters played several instruments and Tontine sang to the harpsichord. Monsieur le Duc was also among their admirers. One summer's day when the sisters were bathing at the Porte Saint Bernard a quarrel arose between them and the wife of a councillor who, they considered, had insulted them. They appealed to Monsieur le Duc, who was bathing nearby. 'Mes Dames', he replied, 'je veux bien partager vos plaisirs, mais non pas vos querelles' ('My ladies, I am happy to participate in your pleasures, but not in your quarrels').[63] Their portraits were painted many times; a description survives from the 1850s when a pair were seen in a house belonging to descendants of the sisters:

Assez peu couverte d'une draperie bleue la blonde Doguine tient sur ses genoux un amour en cocquet déshabillé. Les oiseaux chers à Vénus, deux colombes, folâtrent dans les bras de *l'enfant terrible* ou volettent aux pieds de la belle. Tontine, la brune, les bras et le sein nus, sort d'un nuage de brocart rouge; elle est coiffée comme Mme. de Montespan; les deux boucles des tempes lui tombent bas sur les joues; sa gorge porte en sautoir un grand collier de perles embellies de pendeloques de diamants. Devant elle, un autre amour, aussi en costume un peu *risqué*, lui lance un regard tendre et ouvre un cahier de musique où on lit ces mots: *Sarabande de Mlle. Loyson.*[64]

(Scantily draped in blue the blonde Doguine is portrayed with a flirtatious and scantily clad Cupid on her knee. Two doves, birds dear to Venus, sport in the arms of the incorrigible infant or flutter at the feet of the beauty. Tontine, the brunette, arms and breast bare, emerges from a cloud of red brocade; her hair is dressed like Madame de Montespan; the two curls at her temples fall on her cheeks; a grand necklace of pearls embellished with pendants of diamonds stretches cross-wise on her throat. Before her, another Cupid, also in a somewhat basic costume, throws her a tender glance and opens a book of music where one reads the words: *Sarabande de Mlle. Loyson.*)

63. Madame Du Noyer, *Lettres historiques et galantes*, I, p. 17.
64. Jacques Replat, *Voyage au long cours sur le Lac d'Annecy*, p. 75.

Charles Rivière Dufresny: engraving by F. Jouillain
after Charles-Antoine Coypel, from the frontispiece to
Oeuvres de Monsieur Du Freny, Paris, 1731

The author speculates as to whether these portraits are by
Largillière, Mignard or Rigaud, but since the description of
Tontine exactly fits an engraving by Bouys of a portrait by de
Troy (which survives) they must surely be by that artist.[65] The

65. I am grateful to Davitt Moroney for sight of the engraving and for
general discussion on the Loyson sisters.

portrait of Doguine has not been traced. Regnard wrote of Tontine (who was exactly the same age as Couperin and an excellent harpsichordist):

> Qu'elle est charmante
> Avec les accents de sa voix!
> Ou quand une corde touchante
> Parle tendrement sous ses doigts,
> Qu'elle est charmante.[66]

(How charming she is, with her expressive voice! Or when an expressive string speaks tenderly under her fingers.)

Other friends who met at Grillon were Monsieur le Duc and the Prince de Conti as well as people from the theatre, and presumably musicians as well. Regnard claimed that 'Ici le moindre domestique a du talent pour la musique'[67] ('Here the meanest servant has a talent for music').

Charles Dufresny

Charles Dufresny was twenty years older than Couperin. He was said to be descended from Henri IV, a king whose amorous adventures were responsible for quite a proportion of the population. For this reason Dufresny's family held positions at the court, and his was that of Huissier ordinaire de la Chambre du Roi. As a boy he gained favour with the young Louis XIV with his jokes and mimicry, and with his songs, for which he wrote both words and music. Titon Du Tillet says that he understood music perfectly and his lively and amusing portraits of almost all the different characteristics of mankind were 'd'un goût nouveau',

66. Joseph Guyot, *Regnard à Grillon*, p. 86.
67. Guyot, *Regnard à Grillon*, p. 12.

which is exactly what he says of Couperin's *Pièces de Clavecin*. Possibly Dufresny was one of Couperin's inspirations.[68] He knew how to cut people down to size and portray them in delightfully comic thumb-nail sketches. He also knew how to design *jardins à l'anglais* before the English themselves did, and is said to have had a hand in the park at Versailles. When the wind changed at court with Madame de Maintenon's rule, Dufresny sold his position of Huissier. He held open house in Paris and indulged in costly fantasies. The King, who always protected him, felt powerless to enrich him. To escape arrest he had three different dwellings but, a frenetic gambler, he spent most of his time in the gambling dens, where he is said to have met Regnard. The two collaborated amicably for several years but fell out over *Le Joueur*, a case of plagiarism or jealousy or both. The exact facts of the quarrel are not clear.[69]

It has been suggested that Couperin's *Concert* entitled *Dans le Goût Théâtral* must have originated as orchestral music for the theatre.[70] The overture opens with the treble and bass in different keys. This overture, and a very beautiful 'sad air' in the *Concert*, were very possibly originally incidental music for Dufresny's *Les Mal-assortis*, which comes from Gherardi's collection and to which Couperin refers in the *Sixteenth Ordre*. The rest of the *Concert dans le Goût Théâtral* may also have been music for these plays. Couperin's sense of the theatre is revealed in the way in which he planned his *ordres*. Even the long, and at first glance disorganized, *ordres* in *Book I* reveal, on closer understanding, a

68. Titon Du Tillet, *Le Parnasse françois*, pp. 596, 664.

69. The information on Dufresny is taken from the introduction by Jean Vic to his edition of Charles Dufresny, *Les Amusemens sérieux et comiques*.

70. Peter Holman, 'An orchestral suite by François Couperin?'.

carefully arranged sequence of contrasted pieces (see the essay on Architecture below).

The preoccupation of the Italian theatre with the two sides of life had equal importance for Couperin. This manifests itself not only in his portraits of ladies of dubious morals, but in one of his finest pieces, *Les Amusemens* from the *Seventh Ordre*. Gherardi in the preface to his *Théâtre* could almost be speaking for Couperin:

> Je passe sous silence la satyre fine et délicate, la connoissance parfaite des mœurs du siècle, les expressions neuves et detournées, l'enjouement, l'esprit; en un mot, tout le sel et toute la vivacité dont tous les dialogues de ce Recueil sont remplis.

> (I will pass in silence over the refined and subtle satire, the perfect understanding of the manners of the century, the new and diverting expressions, the humour, the wit; in a word, all the salt and all the spirit with which the dialogues in this collection abound.)

In order to grasp the all-embracing view of human life that Couperin's portraits reveal and his disappointment at the lack of recognition and understanding this received, it is necessary to look at the *Pièces de Clavecin* in their entirety.

JC

Aspects of the literary scene

The court

ONE OF THE MOST ENDURING images of Louis XIV is of the great patron of the arts and lover of the theatre, the man who supported Molière, who awarded Racine and Boileau posts as *Historiographes du Roi*, and the person responsible for inviting a troupe of Italian actors to establish itself permanently in Paris, the monarch whose great entertainments called on the talents of the most gifted writers, musicians, dancers and stage-designers of his day. The atmosphere of the last three decades of his reign was, however, very different. The death of the Queen in 1683 seems to mark the last obstacle to the influence of the pious Madame de Maintenon, who would become his morganatic wife; and the revocation of the Edict of Nantes in 1685 was a turning point, the end of the era of religious tolerance begun by Henri IV, and the beginning of the domination of extreme conservative Catholic views, represented most famously by Bossuet. Although theatrical performances at court continued, the Abbé de Choisy was able to write in 1686 that the King no longer attended them.[1]

1. See Virginia Scott, *The 'Commedia dell'Arte' in Paris*, pp. 248–9. For an interesting view of these developments and the way changes of attitude during the reign of Louis XIV and beyond are reflected in the arts, particularly ballet, see Georgia J. Cowart, *The Triumph of Pleasure: Louis XIV and the Politics of Spectacle*.

The Abbé de Choisy

François-Timoléon, Abbé de Choisy (1644–1724), reflected this change from worldliness to austerity in the court more spectacularly than most, and, since he may well appear in the *Pièces de Clavecin*, he is worthy of some attention here. He was a noted transvestite and active bisexual, who appears to have come out of women's clothing just long enough to take his orders to become an abbé before reverting to his previous habits. He called himself Madame de Sancy at one stage, even taking church services in female attire, and would later call himself the Comtesse Des Barres. One of his specialities was to use his female attire to deceive mothers into entrusting their daughters to him, thus allowing him to seduce them, although he also seems to have used it as an aid in the initial stages of the seduction of unsuspecting men, indeed an example of *les goûts réunis*. Nevertheless, as a result of his lifestyle, he found himself hounded first out of Paris and then out of France. Eventually, though, he returned to his native country, and at about the time of the death of the Queen, the event which marked the beginning of real power for Madame de Maintenon, he suffered an illness which seems to have brought about a change of heart and behaviour. In 1685 he joined the Chevalier de Chaumont's ambassadorial mission to Siam, and in the same year he took full holy orders to become a priest. His account of the voyage to Siam even earned him a place in the Académie Française. Neither did his early lifestyle prevent him from publishing works of religious devotion, although his memoirs are the literary work for which he is best-known today. Given the erotic significance of the musette (which Jane Clark points out on p. 161), it is difficult to imagine that he is not the subject of the *Muséte de Choisi*, but that erotic reference also indicates a strong satirical intent, suggesting that Couperin regarded the change of character that coincided so closely with the change in attitude at court as pure hypocrisy – for Couperin he remains the sexual being he had always been, a classic example of the false prude.

The Italians

Clearly, the new-found piety of the monarchy was open to satire, and although the Italian actors were not the only producers of satirical material during this period, they were the ones most famously to incur the wrath of the monarch when they were 'expelled' from France in 1697. We might note, however, that the term should be taken with a pinch of salt: certainly the troupe was disbanded, never to be re-formed, but a significant number of the actors remained in Paris, where they found alternative employment.[2]

The first appearance of an Italian troupe in France was as early as 1571, and regular visits were made, always at the invitation of the monarch, until in 1662 a period of residence began that would be interrupted only by that expulsion of 1697. These troupes all performed the type of theatre known today as *commedia dell'arte*, the improvised form developed in Renaissance Italy.

Their performances were, however, far from being the free-for-alls that could be suggested by the use of improvisation. They had as their basis reasonably detailed scenarios, most commonly using the standard Plautine plot, in which young lovers enlist the aid of servants to overcome parental opposition to their affection. These scenarios would be used to give at least a semblance of coherence to a spectacle based largely on pre-existing comic routines (*lazzi*, as they were known) and set-piece speeches, whether comic or

2. See Scott, *The 'Commedia dell'Arte' in Paris*, passim.

romantic, that could serve in a variety of different contexts. It seems likely that even the linking dialogue, although initially improvised, would have become relatively stable after a period of rehearsal. And perhaps most significantly, the actors always played the same characters, the *tipi fissi*: lovers, lecherous old men, boastful but cowardly soldiers, and the comic *zanni* (the word is, of course, the source of the English word 'zany'), whether the intelligent and witty first *zanni* or the stupid second *zanni*. The comic characters played masked and in traditional stylized costumes, and not only did each actor carry the same name and costume from play to play, the most successful of these archetypes were passed from actor to actor, and, in some cases, remain famous even today: Arlecchino became Arlequin in French and Harlequin in English, and if Pierrot, whose French name reflects his invention by the Italians in France, was for a long time to be found in Pierrot shows at the end of the pier in British holiday resorts, Pulcinella, who became the puppet Polichinelle in France, was, and occasionally still is, to be found on the beach in the form of Mr Punch.

Such a type of entertainment clearly did not lend itself to the sort of coherent satire that can be produced by a single hand, neither did the traditional Italian framework invite specific satirical comment on the French régime, and, although it certainly did lend itself to topical and scathing ad-libs, the actors were clearly sensitive to just how far they could go: even in the 1690s, when clerical opposition to the theatre became particularly pronounced, there appear to be very few examples of censorship for reasons of political or personal satire. On the other hand, the Italians did find themselves, towards the end of their stay, in trouble for obscenity: in January 1696 the King apparently threatened to expel them if they did not expunge all obscenity from their performances.[3] Although Angelo Costantini as Mezzetin, who appears to have joined the troupe only in 1686,[4] was apparently one of the worst offenders, it still seems probable that these complaints reflected the changing moral climate rather than any change of practice among the Italians.

The Italian theatre was very much to the taste of the court audiences, and remained so; even though, as we are about to see, the repertoire of the troupe became more and more French, they never abandoned the Italian comedy completely, and it was this that they invariably performed at court. A further indication of royal enthusiasm for the traditional comedy, and of the fact that the dismissal of the troupe rankled with certain members of the royal family, was provided after the death of Louis XIV, when the Regent, Philippe d'Orléans, lost no time in inviting a replacement troupe back to Paris under the directorship of Luigi Riccoboni: the King died on 29 August 1715, and the new Italian troupe made its début in France on 18 May 1716, which suggests that the matter was rather high on the Regent's list of priorities. Despite their subvention from the King, however, the Italians had to make money from the town audience too, and Italian comedy was rather less to their taste, so things had to change in order to appeal equally to them. *Le Régal des dames* (1668) seems to have marked a turning point both in its use of music, something that would increasingly be seen as typically Italian despite its never having been a particular feature of the *commedia*, and in Arlequin's adoption for the first time of the travesty of a ridiculous *marquis*. The foppish *marquis* was a characteristic figure in the theatre of Molière, with whom the Italians were sharing a theatre at this

3. See Scott, *The 'Commedia dell'Arte' in Paris*, pp. 325–6.
4. See Scott, *The 'Commedia dell'Arte' in Paris*, p. 267.

time, so, although this development represents a general move in the direction of a satirical approach to contemporary French society, it can hardly be seen as daring: even though direct satire of the court was out of the question, the *marquis* seem to have been seen as fair game by everyone.[5]

It is only with the engagement of French authors that we begin to find a more satirical content in the Italian repertoire.[6] In the early 1680s, when French contributions first appeared, they were not complete plays, but scenes inserted into Italian scenarios. Nevertheless, the very fact of their being texts which were authored and had to be pre-learned represented a major change of approach for the Italians. In due course these French scenes would grow into coherent plays which left very little room for Italian improvisation. Virginia Scott suggests that this may not only represent an increasing attempt to appeal to the French bourgeois audience, but may also derive from the fact that, after the death of the great Arlequin Domenico Biancolelli (known as Dominique) in 1688, and his replacement by the less gifted Evaristo Gherardi, the troupe was less able to improvise to its previous standard: 'The shortage of charismatic performers must have created the void the writers rushed to fill.'[7]

The satire introduced by these writers, of whom the most important are Regnard and Dufresny, is typically French, even

5. See Molière, *L'Impromptu de Versailles* (1663), scene i.
6. The contributions of French authors to the repertoire of the Italian theatre are collected in *Le Théâtre italien; ou, le Recueil général de toutes les comédies et scènes françoises jouées par les comédiens du roy, pendant tout le temps qu'ils ont été au service*, ed. Evaristo Gherardi.
7. Scott, *The 'Commedia dell'Arte' in Paris*, p. 387.

Evaristo Gherardi: engraving by Gérard Edelinck after
Joseph Vivien, from the 1741 edition of Gherardi's *Théâtre Italien*

The Latin inscription reads: Hic ille est Italam (Dominici morte) Cadentem
| Scenam, cui soli sustinuisse Decus. | Hic ille est Italam (Fato cogente)
jacintem | Scenam, cui soli restituisse Decus

(This is he who, upon the death of Dominique, had the honour of sus-
taining the Italian theatre in its fall. This is he who, as fate would have it,
had the honour of restoring the Italian theatre at its lowest point [translation
by Peter Bavington])

Moliéresque. Their *Les Chinois* (1692) is as good an example as any, and perhaps, given Couperin's interest in it, worth spending a little time on. This comedy in a prologue and, unusually, four acts[8] concerns the efforts of Octave to prevent the father of his beloved Isabelle from marrying her to one of four rival suitors. Since the father has not previously met any of these suitors – a country gentleman, a doctor, a major and a French actor – Arlequin will impersonate each in turn in such a way as to discredit them. Each impersonation takes up an act, and the play ends with the allegorical character of the Parterre (the Groundlings) declaring the Italian actor Octave to be a more fitting spouse for Isabelle than the French actor impersonated by Arlequin. Although the plot itself is a variant on the typical Italian scenario, and the lapse into the allegorical at the end is a fantasy element that would certainly not be found in French classical comedy, it is difficult to find any vestige of the traditional Arlequin in the impersonations. They rely on the standard satirical technique of exaggeration, with much less use of the burlesque element provided by the character's inability to carry off an accurate impersonation than we would expect from other Arlequins before and after Gherardi. The doctor in particular,

8. French plays of the neo-classical period were normally written in one, three or five acts. The more acts, the more serious we would expect the play to be, and the five-act structure was generally reserved for tragedy or high comedy (*comédie noble*), genres that the audience would have expected to find only at the Théâtre Français. Regnard and Dufresny's structure is certainly not a five-act comedy pretending to be something else (the allegorical prologue is precisely that, not a first act in disguise), so their choice of prologue and four acts is not a gesture of modesty; writing for the Italians, they must have felt that they could be relaxed enough about the rules not to shoe-horn their four-acts-worth of material into three acts, as they really should have done to be classically correct.

with his Latin jargon, could have come straight from Molière, which is particularly disconcerting since he has the distinctly un-Moliéresque characteristic of being Chinese. The fact that he and his followers, who appear only in the second act, provide the only justification for the title, makes it all the more surprising that there should have been no attempt to inject any oriental characteristics into his dialogue: the title, and perhaps also the very superficial orientalism that inspires it, seem to have been a somewhat cynical marketing ploy aimed at exploiting the audience's taste for the exotic.

The impersonation of the French actor represents the sort of parody of one theatre by another already found in Molière's *Impromptu de Versailles* (1663), which would become almost obsessional in the Fair theatres of the early eighteenth century, but perhaps it is also a piece of self-referential comedy of the sort that became popular with the Italians, since Catherine Biancolelli, who played Colombine, had contracted a not-altogether-successful marriage in 1685 with the French actor Pierre Lenoir de La Thorillière[9]: Colombine, unsurprisingly under the circumstances, is of the opinion that an Italian actor is a much better bet. Jane Clark rightly suggests (p. 198) that Couperin's interest in this particular play may derive from the fact that it concludes with the marriage of Isabelle, a French character in this play, to Octave, an Italian, thus dramatizing his own desire for *les goûts réunis*.

This should not, however, be taken to indicate that Regnard and Dufresny necessarily intended to make such an idealistic polemical point. The concept of *goûts réunis* was no less possible in the theatre than in music – the very fact that the companies were so ready to steal each other's ideas proves as much

9. His sister Thérèse was the wife of Dancourt (see below).

– but the economic rivalries between them, caused by the need to compete for audiences and to justify the royal subvention paid for the provision of a certain type of theatrical entertainment, meant that each theatre was anxious to prove both its differences from and its superiority to its rivals. In many respects the text of the play seems designed to underplay the union of the French and the Italian that Couperin, for his part, seems to have found so appealing. Certainly the name of Isabelle's father, Roquillard, is unusual in the Théâtre Italien and obviously French, and when he says that Isabelle wants to marry an Italian, his servant Pierrot comments: 'Ne donnez point votre fille à cette nation-là' ('Don't give your daughter to that nation').[10] But other French elements are confined to indications that the scene is set in Paris: the use of a French setting to keep the French audience interested was usual in the plays written for the Italians by French authors. On the other hand, Roquillard's daughter is Isabelle, her companion Colombine, and his two servants Pierrot and Marinette – all standard figures of the Théâtre Italien. And when we get to the last act, the situation becomes even more complex: the actor who played Octave is known to have had poor French – his character says as much in the play, when he comments[11] that he cannot defend the cause of the Italian actors properly because he cannot speak French well enough, something that was true in real terms as well as in the fiction of the play. But then it is Colombine – a French character in the play – who takes up his defence (on the grounds that she was once servant to an Italian actor), rather than his own servant Mezzetin. Although Colombine is, in terms of the fiction of the play, French, and is only representing the Italians,

10. I, i.
11. IV, i.

she is, in reality, a member of the Italian troupe herself. It is, therefore, significant that Arlequin, in his guise as French actor, immediately slips into referring to the Italians as *vous* (second-person plural) when he is speaking to her. Shortly afterwards, she begins using the *nous* form (first-person plural) to talk about the Italian troupe, and then, even more significantly, replies to a criticism that the Italians are mules by saying that mules are sterile, '& tout le monde sait que Marinette [also playing a French character in the play] & Colombine ont des enfants tous les neuf mois' ('and everyone knows that Marinette and Colombine have children every nine months'),[12] and a stage direction has Le Parterre 'montrant Marinette grosse' ('indicating Marinette, who is pregnant'),[13] obviously a reference to reality at the time, rather than the fiction of the play. In other words, there is a constant blurring of the levels of illusion and reality. The Italian actors never just played a part, in the way that we would normally understand it: because the same actor tended to play the same character, the archetypal force of this character became very strong. So, as with Octave here, the actor is playing an archetype that has an existence outside the confines of this single play. In the case of the Italians who play a French family in *Les Chinois*, there is a sense in which the actor plays the archetype, and then the archetype plays a character – something that is seen more obviously in the prologue, where Colombine plays Apollo, Arlequin Thalia, etc. It is for this reason that Regnard and Dufresny can make Colombine a French servant and still refer to her quite openly as an Italian actress.

12. IV, ii.
13. IV, ii.

67

Because of the strength of the various conventions at work in this form of theatre, this sort of unlikely mixture is very common, suggesting perhaps that the conventions and archetypes had a stronger impact on the audience than the details of the individual plot. Hence, the Italian actor Octave would always be the fitting spouse for the Italian archetype Isabelle, even if she is playing a French woman, since their archetypal characters are traditionally young lovers, and with the appropriateness typical of comedy, he is the one she marries in the end: Arlequin, as one of the *zanni*, would always be an inappropriate spouse for Isabelle, whether disguised as a Frenchman or not. In this context, we can see that the most important function of Pierrot's comment that you should not marry your daughter to an Italian, or Colombine's contention that she knows about the Italian theatre only because she has worked for an Italian actor, is as comic in-jokes relying on the audience's knowledge of the actors outside the play, rather like the references to Marinette's pregnancy and Colombine's rocky marriage to a French actor.

Nevertheless, even if, as I suspect, Regnard and Dufresny were not setting out to make a polemical point about the desirability of uniting the French and Italian styles in the theatre, a suspicion that is perhaps confirmed by the very different style that Regnard in particular adopted for his plays for the French troupe, there is in *Les Chinois* a very rich and complex mixture of French and Italian which Couperin could have found particularly congenial.

The first part of the prologue to *Les Chinois* raises other interesting issues. It makes use of burlesque techniques by giving down-to-earth attitudes to mythological figures, and further reduces their credibility by having them played by archetypal characters of the opposite sex in travesty: as we have already noted, the god Apollo is played by Colombine, and Thalia, muse of comedy, by Arlequin. They are approached by a little girl (played by Pierrot), who complains that her mother will not let her go to the Italian theatre because of the obscenities she may hear there. The double standard of the mother, in taking enjoyment herself in something she finds improper for her daughter, is clear (although which parent could plead 'not guilty' to it?). But it goes further: if she objects specifically to the word *cocu* ('cuckold'), it is made clear that this is because she has herself made her husband one, and there are even hints that the little girl too may already be of easy virtue: she is too young, she says, to go to the Bois de Boulogne (which had the same reputation then as now), but she does go on to the ramparts (which are clearly no better). At the conclusion of the discussion Apollo promises to speak firmly to the actors, but Thalia suggests that in changing things to keep one person happy, he risks upsetting a lot more.

This scene will obviously remind us of the King's forthcoming complaints about obscenity in the Italian theatre in 1696, so clearly it was not a new issue – unless, of course, the prologue printed in Gherardi's 1700 collection represents a reworked version responding specifically to the events of 1696. The little girl's mother reminds us of the young ladies in Molière who are 'plus chastes des oreilles que de tout le reste du corps' (whose 'ears are more chaste than the whole of the rest of their bodies'),[14] but perhaps also, with hindsight, of the Italians' *Fausse Prude*, of whom more anon. Might Regnard and Dufresny's contemporaries also have been reminded of the double standards of the woman who, having been married to the playwright and novelist Scarron and then mistress to the King, was seen as chiefly responsible for the court's move towards religious orthodoxy and the affectation of virtue, that is to say Madame de Maintenon? Certainly she was

14. *La Critique de 'L'École des femmes'* (1663), scene iii.

the woman most likely to complain of the obscenity that was enjoyed by everyone else.

It is to the opening stage direction of Regnard and Dufresny's play that Couperin's piece entitled *Les Chinois* makes specific reference:

> Le théâtre représente le mont Parnasse, avec Apollon & les muses du mont. Sur le sommet paraît un âne ailé, représentant Pégase. On entend un concert ridicule de plusieurs instruments comiques, qui est interrompu par l'âne qui se met à braire. [15]

> (The stage represents Mount Parnassus, with Apollo and the muses who live there. A winged ass, representing Pegasus, appears on the summit. A ridiculous ensemble of several comic instruments is heard, and is interrupted by the ass, which begins to bray.)

The piece begins with music which, despite suggesting by both its slow tempo and dotted rhythms the opening of a French overture, is a loure, a dance often used satirically by Couperin, and later by Rameau, and it also contains the motif of a braying ass. The music that supplants this is not the French fugue we might expect, but music in a much more Italianate mode, which manages, even on the harpsichord, to carry suggestions of the 'instruments comiques' of the stage direction. Jane Clark points out (p. 200) that this piece sits awkwardly on the keyboard, suggesting that it is an arrangement of music originally written for orchestral forces and intended as incidental music for the play. In fact, it would make a very appropriate overture – the braying ass and the 'concert ridicule' are both there, and the form is at least reminiscent of the standard French overture. Moreover, what it is introducing is an allegorical prologue of the type that was most commonly in use at the Opéra, but here burlesqued in the Italian

15. Prologue, i.

70

manner. So the portentous music in the French style of the loure that begins the piece is satirized both by the inclusion of the motif of the braying ass and by the fact that it is supplanted by music in the Italian manner (particularly ridiculous in its effect if played on silly instruments), in just the same way that the Opéra-style scene of Parnassus and the gods is deflated by the braying Pegasus and the playing of the gods by Italian archetypes. So here Couperin's use of the *goûts réunis* is a perfect foil to the piece it appears to have been intended to introduce.

My earlier mention of *La Fausse Prude* brings us to the matter of the Italians' expulsion. The usual story suggests that the Italians commissioned a French version of an Italian scenario, *La finta matrigna* (*The False Mother-in-law*), and that this version, in order to make clear its satire of Madame de Maintenon, was to be entitled *La Fausse Prude*. The play was advertised, but it is not entirely clear whether it was performed or whether the Italians were expelled before they could bring it to the stage.[16] If this were true, it would put the troupe at the forefront of radical satire of the establishment, but unfortunately, despite the frequent repetitions of the tale, its accuracy remains uncertain. There is general confusion over whether *La Fausse Prude* ever existed; it has certainly never been found. There is not even any evidence that the Italian original, *La finta matrigna*, was performed: the last performances by the troupe appear to have been the début piece of Maria Teresa d'Orsi in the role of Spinette, an Italian play recorded under the French title *Spinette lutin amoureux*, an ill-

16. Even if this story were to turn out to be authentic, there is certainly no evidence that matters went any further than this, although I have seen a retelling of the tale that suggests that the play was actually performed in the presence of Madame de Maintenon, a clear example of a good story taking on a life of its own quite independently of the truth.

timed début if ever there was one. Yet, whilst many sources that we would expect to be aware of performances of *La Fausse Prude* either demonstrate no knowledge of it at all or dismiss it as a rumour, both Saint Simon and the Duchesse d'Orléans (the latter writing some twenty-three years after the event, and neither saying they had seen it themselves) claim that it was performed with success, whilst the Italian actor Costantini, in 1729 and hence even longer after the event, contradicted this version when he told Gueullette that the play was advertised but not performed. He also commented that the title *La Fausse Prude* was drawn from a satire of Madame de Maintenon published in Amsterdam, but, like the play, no trace of this has ever been found. Perhaps a play was advertised, perhaps not; perhaps it was even performed, perhaps not; perhaps what was performed was the Italian play *La finta matrigna* re-titled or sub-titled with the inflammatory title, but perhaps not. Certainly, given the lack of clarity, it seems most plausible that the whole *Fausse-Prude* affair was no more than a pretext for the expulsion, but then what was the real reason? Bruce Griffiths' contention that 'the King saw in the Théâtre Italien the last surviving uncontrolled source of very public satire of his régime'[17] is appealing, but it does not seem to be borne out by Virginia Scott's evidence that they were more frequently in trouble for obscenity than for any political satire. Could it be that the King eventually lost patience on that very matter of obscenity? Could it be that he had simply had enough of paying 15,000 *livres* a year (or 18,000, according to some) to a troupe he was no longer interested in watching? A surprising number of those who wrote about the expulsion at the time commented on the amount of

17. Bruce Griffiths, 'Sunset: from *commedia dell'arte* to *comédie italienne*', p. 104.

money the King would save, whether or not they had any knowledge of the rumours about *La Fausse Prude*; his kingdom was now, after all, bankrupt, and Scott suggests that by 1697 he might well have fallen behind with the payments to the tune of 99,000 *livres*. It may be the most banal explanation, but it also seems the most plausible.[18]

The Théâtre Français

French audiences of the seventeenth and eighteenth centuries had curious double standards in their attitudes to what was acceptable in different theatres. At the Théâtre Français, where the classical rules of the *bienséances* were traditionally observed, they might affect outrage at the merest hint of obscenity, whilst they would cheerfully enjoy the real thing at the Théâtre Italien and, later, the Fair theatres. We would not, therefore, expect to find the sort of risqué material that was traditional in the *commedia* being employed by the French actors. Paradoxically, though, when it came to real life, whilst Italian actors prided themselves on being respectable members of society, the French actors generally deserved the reputation they had for loose living.

Dancourt

The Dancourts were no exception to this, a fact that is perhaps not totally irrelevant, since the appearance in the *ordres* of not

18. See Scott, *The 'Commedia dell'Arte' in Paris*, pp. 326–31, on this whole matter. Some relevant documents are reproduced in English in *French Theatre in the Neo-Classical Era, 1550–1789*, ed. William D. Howarth, pp. 304–6.

only Dancourt himself, but also his wife and both daughters, could indicate a personal rather than artistic interest on the part of Couperin. Although both an effective actor and a gifted writer for the Théâtre Français, Dancourt (1661–1725) could not always be relied on either to meet deadlines or to appear at meetings. He was frequently in debt, and could also be violent towards his actress wife Thérèse, and, whilst it must be said that his jealousy had ample justification, he was far from being a paragon of marital fidelity himself. His daughters Mimi and Manon were famous in the latter part of the seventeenth century as child actresses, and, although Manon left the theatre when she married, Mimi subsequently went on to have a successful adult career.

As an actor in the French troupe, Dancourt was one of the few significant playwrights of his and the next generation to write for only one of the rival theatres. His best-known play, perhaps rightly considered his masterpiece, and undoubtedly one of the finest comedies written between the death of Molière and the arrival on the scene of Marivaux, was also his first major success, *Le Chevalier à la mode* (1687). This play is untypical of most of his work in being a five-act comedy; it is generally agreed that he lacked the ability to structure a play of this length, and that the structural tautness of this work is to be attributed to his collaborator, Saint-Yon. Most of his other plays, the *dancourades* as they became known, are in one act, or at most three, and are characterized by a certain looseness of structure, often with much use of music and dance elements. We have already noted that the Italians had begun to introduce music and dance into their theatre as a way of attracting audiences, and the introduction of similar elements into his shorter plays by Dancourt could be seen as an attempt by the French troupe to cash in on their success. So perhaps here too we have an example of *goûts réunis*, but it is again born of rivalry rather than admiration, even if imitation remains the sincerest form of flattery.

Although the *dancourades* cover a wide range of subjects, milieux and sources, anyone who knows only *Le Chevalier à la mode* will still have a good sense of the characteristics that make Dancourt a great author. He has a gift for apparently spontaneous, even realistic, dialogue, and a keen interest in contemporary life: many of the *dancourades* take specific events as their starting point, and the depiction of contemporary manners and attitudes is one of his strongest suits. Hence, much of his comedy is satirical, but in a different way from that of the Italians, with their post-Moliéresque use of caricature and burlesque. Certainly Dancourt's characters are exaggerated – that is in the nature of any satire – but that exaggeration is much more restrained than that of either his rivals or his illustrious predecessor. Consequently, the characters often seem unpleasant rather than simply foolish, and the satire lies principally in depicting on stage characters and attitudes that the establishment would prefer not to be made public.

These last decades of the Sun King's reign were a time of financial instability, and money and rank (both of them often linked in the plays to sex) are frequent preoccupations of the unpleasant characters in Dancourt's witty but cynical comedies. From the devious impoverished nobleman of *Le Chevalier à la mode,* who seduces older women for their money, to the unscrupulous financiers of his last major play, *Les Agioteurs* (1710), his work is a portrait gallery of the various types and obsessions of his time. André Blanc writes of one of Dancourt's most cynical works, *La Femme d'intrigues* (1692), that it was the first time that the seamy side of the *grand siècle* had been shown on stage, but there are surely traces of it in many more of his works.[19] Interestingly, the only time he appears to have had his wrists metaphorically slapped by the King was over the satirical portraits of the Duke of Savoy and the Elector of Bavaria, both at the time enemies of France, in *Le Carnaval de Venise* (1690): Louis was apparently so touchy about the dignity of kingship that even enemy princes were considered above satire.

Les Visionnaires

The apparent reference to Desmarets de Saint-Sorlin's play *Les Visionnaires* (1637) in the *Twenty-fifth Ordre* is surprising for being the only literary reference that is not contemporary; it is true that its final performance at the Théâtre Français was as late as 1695, but performances had already become infrequent, and it was by then a singularly old-fashioned play. Its title is the first recorded use of the word *visionnaire* as a noun, but by the late seventeenth century it was familiar enough to make it possible that Couperin's use of it was not a reference to the play. Although it is not impossible that, as Jane Clark suggests (pp. 192–3), the piece has connections with the depiction of Rosicrucians as 'seers', we need to be very clear what we mean by that word. For Desmarets *visionnaires* are madmen (and women), people who cannot differentiate between fantasy and reality, and that is still the principal meaning of the word in the late seventeenth century and

19. Blanc, *F. C. Dancourt (1661–1725). La Comédie française à l'heure du Soleil couchant*, p. 49. This is the most important study of Dancourt's work produced to date.

into the eighteenth.[20] In 1671 it also acquired the meaning of 'one who has visions', but it was perhaps more often used in a pejorative sense than as a neutral expression of fact. The more extended meanings given to the word 'seer' in modern English, that of a prophet or someone with a heightened understanding of the nature of things, would not be attached to the French word *visionnaire* until the mid-nineteenth century.

The music itself does not provide us with a clear-cut answer to the problem. The first section, in the Masonic key of E flat,[21] certainly seems serious in intent. But why then should Couperin have chosen for his title a word that would most readily be understood in a pejorative sense? The quick section which follows is more difficult to pin down. It is perhaps not impossible that the music is intended to have a character of madness, but this is far from certain. Is Couperin perhaps playing with the duality implied by the title, in which the first section is an un-ironic depiction of his victims as they see themselves, with the quick second section being intended to deflate and mock the solemnity of their self-image?

Or could the use of the title of Desmarets's play even be intended as a reference to the author himself? Two of the eight *visionnaires* in Desmarets's play, a braggart soldier who is in reality a coward and a self-styled rich man who has no fortune, make

20. For instance, in the first act of the Fair play *Les Trois Commères* of 1723 (*Le Théâtre de la Foire*, IX) a character whose wife wants to trick him into thinking he is imagining things is told by one of her co-conspirators that he is a *visionnaire*; and later, as the weight of evidence against him builds up, he begins to wonder himself if he is a *visionnaire*. In the meantime, a *commissaire* who is convinced by the trick tells him he must be imagining things with the phrase: 'Je crains qu'il n'y ait un peu de vision dans votre fait'.

21. See Jane Clark's remarks on the piece (pp. 192–3).

extravagant claims about themselves that have no basis in truth. Perhaps this is not too far away from our old friend *la fausse prude*, Madame de Maintenon, and the life of Desmarets may provide an example of the same sort of hypocrisy that Couperin seems to have disliked so much in that particular member of the royal family, which has analogies with the conversion of Louis himself from pleasure seeker to devout follower of religion, and which we have already seen satirized in the person of the Abbé de Choisy.

It was during a successful early career as purveyor of entertainments to the Cardinal de Richelieu that Desmarets wrote *Les Visionnaires*. After the death of Richelieu, however, he wrote no more for the theatre, and in the early 1650s he underwent a conversion to extreme religious mysticism. It was just such a conversion that lost Molière his first patron, the Prince de Conti (the father of the Prince de Conti who appears in the *Pièces de Clavecin*), when he similarly saw the light; such a conversion of course necessitated a rejection of the theatre, actors being outlawed by the Catholic church in France. Molière later took revenge by satirizing one of Desmarets's devotional works in the 'Maximes du mariage' of *L'École des femmes* (1662). The ensuing battle doubtless provided the impetus for the creation of the religious hypocrite Tartuffe (in the play of 1664), whose first entrance provides one of literature's most famous examples of false prudishness, and Molière's following play, *Dom Juan* (1665), has been seen as a direct attack on Conti and the hypocrisy of his conversion (as Molière saw it, at least). It is for this that Desmarets is principally remembered today, but it would already have been common knowledge in Couperin's time. Again, the comparison with Madame de Maintenon, and even Louis XIV himself, is irresistible.

Vaudeville, and its uses in popular culture

'Vaudeville' is an unhelpfully slippery word, combining, as it does, an uncertain etymology with a somewhat inconvenient habit of changing its meaning, although it was the original meaning that was still dominant during the period that interests us. A vaudeville is, in its simplest and original meaning, a familiar tune to which new words were written. The tunes came from a wide variety of sources, folk songs, popular songs, dance tunes or melodies from operas or ballets. All that was important was that the tunes were familiar and easily sung. They would be identified by a little tag, the *timbre*, as it was called, which would usually be the most memorable phrase from the lyrics, but could also be a short title – for example 'Réveillez-vous, belle endormie' uses the first phrase of the original words; 'Laire la, laire, lanlaire' is the refrain that ends the original lyric; 'Allons, gai' comes from the middle of the original lyric, but was its most characteristic and memorable phrase; 'Branle de Metz' is the title of a dance tune without words. This *timbre* identifies the tune, but is not generally included in the new words except in the case of refrains, most usually nonsense refrains, which often are retained. Some vaudevilles do have a more pronounced character than others, and this will determine the situations in which they are used, and in others the influence of the original words or of the refrain may be felt to ironic effect.[22] Indeed, in the case of tunes with refrains, authors seemed to delight in writing new lyrics that gave the refrain a new and unexpected meaning (often, although by no means always, adding a vaguely obscene resonance to a previously innocent 'tra-la-la'). Most usually, though, it was the relative

22. Philip Robinson has studied this aspect of the use of vaudeville in 'Les vaudevilles: un médium théâtral'.

neutrality and consequent versatility of the tunes that was exploited, allowing them to be turned to all sorts of situations, and the most popular tunes were used so often that it seems unlikely that any vestige of association with the original text would remain apart from the *timbre* that identified it. Jean-Jacques Rousseau wrote in the article 'Vaudeville' of his *Dictionnaire de musique*: 'L'air des vaudevilles est peu musical; comme on n'y fait attention qu'aux paroles, l'air ne sert qu'à rendre la récitation un peu plus appuyée' ('The tune in a vaudeville is not particularly musical; as it is only the words that people pay attention to, the tune serves simply to make the delivery a little more forceful').[23]

One obvious advantage of the use of vaudeville is that a musical entertainment could be put on with a minimum of effort, for not only did new music not need to be composed, it did not need to be learnt either, a clear bonus for actors who were not really musicians, and something that would come in very handy for the Fair theatres with their rapid turn-over of *opéras-comiques*. But the technique really came into its own to enable a public that could not read music to have instant access to songs, something that was essential both for the writers of satirical songs and, as we shall see, in the early days of the Fair theatres, for all that was needed was that the tune be identified by its *timbre* at the head of the new text.

Subsequently the word would come to be used to refer not to the tunes, but to a play that makes use of these tunes, initially the *opéra-comique* of the Fairs, but in modern French most usually the

23. Quoted by Renée Viollier in *Jean-Joseph Mouret le musicien des grâces*, p. 107. I have studied the wide range of situations in which a selection of popular vaudeville tunes were used by the writers of the first Fair plays in 'Music in the Parisian Fair theatres: medium or message'.

nineteenth-century farces that still used vaudeville, albeit more sparingly. It also came to mean the sort of finale typically used in such plays as performed at the Fairs, where each character sings a verse in turn and then all join in with the chorus, even though these finales usually had specially composed music, and so were generally the only musical number in the play not to be a vaudeville in the original sense: it is in this sense that musicians now most often use the term – famous examples occur at the end of Mozart's *Der Schauspieldirektor* and *Die Entführung aus dem Serail*. And, of course, it was adopted in North America as a synonym for Music Hall.

And the etymology? It has been suggested that it is a corruption of either 'voix de ville' ('voices of the city'), referring to the Parisian origins of the trade in satirical vaudeville songs, or of 'Vaux de Vire', songs of the Valley of Vire (*vaux* is the plural of *val*), referring to the home of Olivier Basselin, one of the most famous writers of these songs, but neither is certain, and it is not impossible that the influence of both is present.

Songwriters

Robert M. Isherwood writes of the songwriters centred on the Pont-Neuf: 'The ancien régime depended greatly on public respect and the songwriters resorted to every form of caustic derision to subvert that respect.'[24] The general principle contained in that remark can also, of course, be applied to the satire we have found in the work of the Italians and of Dancourt, but it was particularly true of the satirical songwriters, since they were the

24. Isherwood, *Farce and Fantasy: Popular Entertainment in Eighteenth-Century Paris*, p. 9.

hardest group to control. Their songs, which were often scatological and obscene as well as satirical, themselves became known as *pont-neufs*. Many songs were bawled out by the songwriter before being sold, but the more scandalous could not be sung in public, and were hidden under the salesman's coat before being sold to passers-by, and consequently the vaudeville technique was essential to allow the purchasers to sing the words to the appropriate tune. The use of a popular melody could also add to the sense of deflation when important personages were being attacked. Many of these verses have a lack of literary sophistication that suggests they were written by the singers themselves, but others must have been written by members of the court, if only because they contain information that could only have been known by members of the nobility. Among those who are known to have contributed to the wealth of *pont-neufs* were the d'Argensons, the Dowager Princesse de Conti, the Duchesse de Bourbon, the Comte de Maurepas and the Comte d'Artois.

The Dancourts, and particularly Dancourt's actress wife Thérèse, were not immune from attack, but the songwriters had more important targets, of whom Bossuet and Madame de Maintenon were among the most popular (or should we say unpopular?). Louis XIV alone seems to have remained relatively immune, while he was alive at least, but this immunity ended with his death and did not extend to his successor Louis XV.

The Fair theatres

During the Renaissance the church had begun to authorize the participation in its celebrations of various entrepreneurs as well as theatrical groups acting the lives of the saints. This grew to a rich mix of acrobats, jugglers, rope-dancers and performing animals, providing entertainment amid the salesmen and quacks of all types – indeed, often an element of performance was used by the entrepreneurs to attract custom. The Dutchman quoted by Jane Clark (pp. 44–5) gives a lively impression of what these Fairs were like.

Plays were performed initially on the back of carts and later on trestle stages, and were often no more than dramatic frameworks to add interest and a sense of unity to acrobatic performances. By the end of the seventeenth century, however, both the major Parisian Fairs, Saint-Germain (held from February to Easter) and Saint-Laurent (from July to September), had purpose-built theatres.

The disbanding of the Italian troupe in 1697 provided the Fair companies with a useful gap in the market, and they began to adopt some of the Italian repertoire, and with it, some of its most characteristic features; hence, although the theatre of the Fairs is largely a home-grown product, it has strong Italian features, most obviously its use of a number of characteristic Italian archetypal characters, chief among them Arlequin. In fact, in *La Querelle des théâtres*, a polemical piece dramatizing the conflicts between the Fair and the established troupes that was first performed in 1718, and so after the arrival of the new Italian company, the Fair is played by Pierrot, the Opéra (at this stage regarded as a friend of the Fairs and depicted in the play as the Fair's cousin) by Arlequin, and Mezzetin, Polichinelle and a Gille[25] are also on the Fair's team, leaving the Italians with only Pantalon and Scapin –

25. Usually spelt 'Gilles', although the use of the indefinite article in this play indicates a shift away from the individual character to something more generic. Clearly the 's' would look anomalous in a case like this where the name has become a singular noun.

the Fairs clearly felt that by this stage they had more right to the Italian archetypes than the Italians themselves.

As the Fair theatres became more successful, they began to attract the attention of the established companies, who used their monopolies to squash the competition; Dancourt, as representative of the Théâtre Français, was one of the most tireless campaigners against the Fair companies. The Fairs retaliated by finding ingenious ways around the law, turning to forms not covered by the monopolies, such as monologues, plays in non-sense languages and mime plays. One solution to the limitations of these forms was for the actors to unroll scrolls during the course of a mime play on which the characters' dialogue was written, and, with the addition of the use of vaudeville, this evolved into one of the most inventive theatrical forms ever devised, the *pièce à écritaux* or placard play. In these plays the actors mimed, but placards containing their dialogue in vaudeville form were lowered from the flies. The band indicated the tune, and the audience sang the dialogue themselves. Obviously the use of vaudeville was essential here, as in the *pont-neufs*, for the audience could clearly be expected to sing only tunes they already knew.

Ingenious as this form was, though, it clearly had its limit-ations, and eventually negotiations with the Opéra, which had begun between 1708 and 1710, would lead to the Fair actors being allowed to sing their own dialogue; thus was born *opéra-comique*. From the outset the rules were bent, with brief spoken inter-jections or remarks being included between musical numbers, but very quickly the proportion of spoken dialogue increased, to produce a form that consisted of a regular alternation of speech and song. Although newly composed music could now be included, this was generally reserved for finales and other special purposes, with the bulk of the music continuing to consist of vaudeville. Whether the decision to continue the use of vaudeville was taken because it made life easier for actors and composers, particularly in view of the often rapid turn-over of material, or because the public liked it is uncertain, but there was probably an element of both. Whatever the reason, this type of *opéra-comique* in vaudevilles was a dominant form at the Fairs for the rest of their existence and even went on to outlive them.

Like both the old and new Italian theatres, the Fairs attracted authors of high quality, among the best and also most indefatigable of whom were Lesage, Fuzelier and d'Orneval; an important later recruit was Alexis Piron, whose preferred composer was none other than Jean-Philippe Rameau. Much of the repertoire of the Fair theatres (although Piron is represented by only a single play)[26] is collected in the ten-volume anthology produced by Lesage and d'Orneval under the title of *Le Théâtre de la Foire; ou, l'Opéra-comique.*[27]

Like the products of the old Italian theatre, the entertainments of the Fairs could be bawdy or even downright obscene, but are far from being uniformly so (the plays in the Lesage and d'Orneval anthology tend, on the whole, to be fairly well-

26. A cut version of *Le Caprice* appears as *Le Mariage du Caprice et de la Folie* in the eighth volume. He is also said to have collaborated with Lesage and d'Orneval on *Les Trois Commères*, the last play in volume nine, but no mention is made on the title page of his contribution.

27. The tenth volume (designated volume IX, part 2) is a supplement edited not by Lesage and d'Orneval, but by Carolet. The best historical source for information about the Fair theatres is the Parfaict brothers' *Mémoires pour servir à l'histoire des spectacles de la foire. Par un acteur forain.* Michèle Venard's *La Foire entre en scène* is a useful and concise modern source. A selection of plays from the Lesage and d'Orneval anthology is available in Derek Connon and George Evans (eds), *Anthologie de pièces du 'Théâtre de la Foire'.*

behaved), and overt satire tended to be limited to attacks on rival theatre companies and the old traditional targets like doctors, lawyers and the *petits-maîtres* or fops, who were the direct descendants of Molière's *marquis*.

So, by the time the play that particularly interests us here, *Le Régiment de la Calotte*, was first performed in 1721, the Fair companies were working in proper theatres with machinery capable of producing elaborate special effects – of which the flying in of Momus in this play is only a relatively unspectacular example – and were employing gifted writers and musicians. Couperin's reference to the play as a *pièce à trétaux*, or trestle play (see p. 173), makes it clear that it is indeed this play from the Fair repertoire that he has in mind, but is certainly not to be taken literally. The term could be used as an insult, but in this particular context it seems to me much more likely that it is simply being used as a synonym for 'Fair play', in the same way that in modern English we continue to use the word pantomime both as a purely factual description of a type of entertainment which has, nevertheless, long since stopped being the mime play implied by the term, and also as an insult when directed against a work from any other theatrical genre. Certainly the quality of the plays in the Lesage and d'Orneval anthology is every bit as good as those in Gherardi's Italian anthology, and their unique amalgam of French and Italian characteristics seems guaranteed to have appealed to Couperin's taste for *goûts réunis*.

The Calotins

As tradition has it, the spoof Régiment de la Calotte was founded in 1702 by Aymon (or Aimon or Hémon), coat-bearer to Louis XIV, and Philippe Emmanuel de La Place de Torsac, an officer of the King's bodyguard, as a protest against the authoritarianism of society towards the end of the reign of Louis XIV under the pervasive influence of Madame de Maintenon. Nevertheless, the regiment's activities continued long after the death of Louis XIV in 1715: as late as 1731 we are told that the Comte de Livry, who, like the regiment's founders, was a man with a position in the royal household ('premier maître d'hôtel du roi'), was proclaimed the new general of the regiment in front of a statue of Bacchus in his chateau of Livry, which purported to be its headquarters.[28] One aspect of the activities of the Calotins, whose regiment was really more of a society or club, was social, but their principal aim, like that of the songwriters of the Pont-Neuf, was satirical. Prospective members had to submit a request in verse, in which they mocked their own faults, proving that they were foolish enough to enter the regiment; but more significant were the commissions (*brevets*) in verse and prose addressed to key establishment figures. Decisions about who was and was not eligible to enter the regiment were made by a committee presided over by Aymon or one of his successors, or, according to more fanciful versions, by the presiding deity of the order, Momus, god of ridicule or mockery – it is from his cap that the regiment takes its name, not the ordinary skullcap usually designated by the word,

28. Livry also participated, from 1731 to 1732, in a series of parties, with the Comte de Caylus, the Comte de Maurepas, the actresses Quinault, Balicourt and Dufresne (Thérèse Dancourt seems to have put in some appearances too), Piron, fulfilling the role of orator, and (probably) the writer of *parades*, Salley, as key participants. The manuscript *Histoire et recueil des Lazzis* (edited by Judith Curtis and David Trott) paints a wonderful picture of these soirées, giving us remarkable insight into the inventiveness of the most elaborate private entertainments at this period, but also showing the close links between the aristocracy and the world of the theatre.

but a skullcap of lead, intended to hold in place what little was left of the wits of the nominee. Like the Fairs and the songwriters, the Calotins on occasion used vaudeville to add musical spice to their creations.[29]

It is difficult to sort fact from fiction in all of this, but the contention that the god Momus presided over meetings indicates that there is certainly some degree of fiction, and the *Mémoires* by Aymon and others should undoubtedly be taken with at least a pinch of salt. Whatever the truth, Henri Duranton shows that the earliest surviving Calotin literature dates not from the reign of Louis XIV, but from as late as 1719, with the period of the regency of Philippe d'Orléans showing the most activity: these texts form a satirical catalogue of the scandals of the time. Although written in the spirit of the Calotins, and often taking the form of *brevets*, these later examples were clearly produced not by any association of Calotins, but by individual authors working on their own initiative. Examples of Calotin literature are to be found by authors as famous as Voltaire and Piron, although the most active was the lesser known François Gacon, one of those credited with authorship of the regiment's *Mémoires*. Many of these later *brevets* and associated pieces were published in anthologies. Whilst this

---

29. See the *Mémoires pour servir à l'histoire de la Calotte* (Basle: 1725), by Jean Aymon, François Gacon, the Abbé de Margon and the Abbé Desfontaines, which were reprinted with joke places and publishers in 1732, 1735 and 1739 (Moropolis: Chez le libraire de Momus à l'enseigne du jésuite démasqué), and 1752 (Aux États Calotins: De l'imprimerie Calotine). Pascale Verèb, *Alexis Piron, poète (1689–1773); ou, la Difficile Condition d'auteur sous Louis XV*, pp. 198–203, has some useful information on Piron's role in the tradition. See also Antoine de Baecque, 'Les éclats du rire: le Régiment de la calotte, ou les stratégies aristocratiques de la gaieté française (1702–1752)'.

body of literature is linked to the traditions of the *pont-neufs* and other satirical literature, just as tradition has it that Louis XIV allowed the continued existence of the original regiment at court because of the relative good humour of its activities, Duranton confirms that later Calotin literature also eschews the more vicious excesses of other satirical forms.[30]

Le Régiment de la Calotte

Le Régiment de la Calotte (1721) is a typical Fair play. It appears in the fifth volume of the Lesage and d'Orneval anthology, where the only indication of authorship is a statement in volume four that all the plays in volumes four and five are by Lesage, Fuzelier and d'Orneval; and it is written in the usual *opéra-comique* blend of vaudeville and spoken dialogue with a finale (a vaudeville finale in the extended meaning of that term) by the violinist and composer Jacques Aubert. Like so many plays of the type, it has the sort of loose-leaf structure in which there is no real plot, but merely an initial premise which is simply a hook on which to hang a series of more-or-less independent scenes. The date of the play places it at the time of the proliferation of later Calotin literature, and this is mentioned in the *avertissement* to the play. It also reminds us of the original tradition, and the plot of the play fits precisely with the earlier fiction of meetings presided over by Momus (a god who also had associations with the Fairs them-

30. See Duranton, 'La très joyeuse et très véridique histoire du Regiment de la Calotte'. Duranton indicates that a collection of Calotin literature is currently in preparation.

selves)[31]: Folly is to prove to him that a number of candidates are foolish enough to be admitted to the regiment. There follows a sequence of satirical scenes in which the mockery of traditional figures is mixed with the satire of characters based on real individuals or events, as indicated in notes in the text.[32] This is characteristic of the Fairs, where even the most fantastic plots still retain clear links with the real world and contemporary concerns. Since Couperin's affections seem to have been mainly for the old Italian company rather than the new, he would presumably have been unconcerned, perhaps even amused, by the fact that, as part of the ongoing battle between the Fair and its rivals, the new Italian troupe appears as one of the real-life ridiculous candidates. More important for the musical interest of the play is the fact that the first candidate is a lawyer, whose folly consists not only of marrying a woman who has gone on to cuckold him, but also in taking her to court about it, thus letting everyone else know what she has done to him. In recognition of his stupidity, Momus appoints him *trompette* (trumpeter or bugler) in the Brigade of Cuckolds, a detail commemorated by Couperin, who puts the trumpet and the call of the cuckoo in his music (see p. 173). The final section of the play, in which the Italians are welcomed into the regiment, is a self-confessed imitation of the similar scene in Molière's *Le Malade imaginaire*, where the central character is welcomed into the faculty of medicine. Like Molière's original,

31. See Connon, *Identity and Transformation in the Plays of Alexis Piron*, pp. 125–6.

32. As well as the attack on the Italian actors mentioned below, there is an episode based on an unnamed but, we are assured, real person who made a bet that it would rain for forty days because it had rained on the feast of Saint Gervais. He lost. He appears here under the name of Monsieur Pluvio.

the ceremony is played out in cod Latin, but uses music much more sparingly and more in the simple taste of the Fairs than that written for Molière by Marc-Antoine Charpentier; Aubert, the composer of the vaudeville finale and so very probably of the rest of the original music too, was a stalwart of the Fairs. If, as I have suggested, the Fairs can be seen to represent *les goûts réunis*, then this final scene is one of the best examples of this in action.

*   *   *

So, satire abounds in the literary creations of the period, some of it traditional, some less so. The types and institutions of the France of Louis XIV and of the Regency come under scrutiny; even individuals as close to the King as his morganatic wife are attacked, and we can find a number of other figures, both real and literary, who like her can be accused of false prudishness. This satire clearly appealed to Couperin, as we can see from his own use of the device in the *Pièces de Clavecin*, but he also shows a taste for literary works that reflect his own interest in *les goûts réunis* by blending the French with the Italian, whether it is French authors writing for Italian actors, the Théâtre Français stealing the use of music and dance that the Italians had made their own, or the unique blend of Italian characters and plots with French actors and authors found at the Fairs. We might add too that, in terms of his literary taste at least, the works that attract his attention suggest that Couperin was certainly no highbrow.

DFC

Frontispiece of Gherardi, *Théâtre italien*, Vol. III, Paris, 1700:
engraving by Jean Audran after Boulogne the younger

THE ARCHITECTURE OF THE *ORDRES*

THE BELIEF that François Couperin was a Freemason is expressed by the Grand Lodge of France in the notes accompanying a centenary recording of *The Magic Flute*.[1] This is possible because, if Edward Corp is right in his suggestion that Couperin worked at the exiled Stuart court at Saint-Germain,[2] he would have been among many Freemasons there (see p. 18).

The type of Freemasonry subscribed to by the Stuarts was ancient, Templar Masonry, and it is also likely that the Bourbon-Condé family, for whom Couperin worked, were Freemasons of this kind. The Duchesse Du Maine formed her own secret Order of the Honey Bee in 1703, with thirty-nine members (see *Les Abeilles, First Ordre*). The honey bee is one of the most common Masonic symbols. The Duchess's order is held by some Masonic historians to have been a parody of a Masonic lodge.[3] She was consumed by ambition for her own family. A carefully chosen group of supporters of her plans, sworn to secrecy, would have been, at the very least, convenient, and was probably a necessity. For all her seemingly frivolous activities, and these were doubtless a helpful cover, she was a serious political force to be reckoned with. This type of lodge, which was surely no parody but a

1. This special and limited edition, with extensive notes on the history of Freemasonry and the Grand Lodge of France, was issued for the centenary of the Grand Lodge in 1994, and uses the recording conducted by Nikolaus Harnoncourt (Teldec, 1990); it is not on general release.

2. Edward Corp, 'François Couperin and the Stuart court'.

3. Paul Naudon, *Freemasonry: A European Viewpoint*, p. 104.

symbolic and practical aid in her subversive activities, pre-dated the Lodges of Adoption that admitted women and is found in circumstances where family loyalties had to be concealed.[4] It is perhaps a mistake to underestimate the traditions of the Condés, who had been *Frondeurs*, and the *Fronde* families are held by some historians to have been Templar Masons.

After the death of Louis XIV the Duchesse Du Maine had a track record of subversion. Apart from her well-known involvement in the Cellamare Conspiracy of 1718–20, a plot to depose the Regent, the Duc d'Orléans, she was suspected by the British government of joining forces with the Jacobites in their plans for an invasion in 1726, by which time she was forty-two. Horatio Walpole, the British Envoy in Paris, in his report to the government, said he thought she had journeyed to Eu in Normandy to be nearer to England. He described her as 'extremely talkative' and said she was 'reckoned to be a lady of Intrigue in Politics, of much knowledge in Poetry and polite learning, of great elegance and fluency in language, and of so much vivacity and wit as to be sometimes a little mad'.[5] Another letter written at the same time by an anonymous agent reported that the Duchess 'maintains secret relations with Bolingbroke [Henry St John, Viscount Bolingbroke, a man with strong Jacobite leanings] and Madame de Villette [Bolingbroke's wife]'. He found her journey to the country 'mysterious' and believed that she wanted to 'enfeeble the Crown of France'.[6] She was still under suspicion in subsequent reports. There is a distinct similarity between the behaviour of the British Royalists during the Commonwealth, the Condé family

4. See Jane Clark, 'Lord Burlington is here', pp. 302–3.
5. British Library, Newcastle Papers, Add. 32747, f. 114, 6 August 1726.
6. Ibid., f. 117.

after the *Fronde*, and the Duchesse Du Maine after the Cellamare Conspiracy: they all retire to their country estates and share a culture of innocent pastoral activities and literature whilst continuing their secret aims.

Olivier Baumont, in a paper delivered at Villecroze in 1995,[7] speculated as to why Couperin called his suites *ordres*. He discussed the Three Orders of Architecture, which of course are the foundations of Freemasonry; although Baumont did not make that connection, it seems very likely that Couperin's position as a Freemason gave him the idea. Freemasons believed that the Three Orders of Architecture were designed by God. The number three, so sacred to Freemasons, probably has significance in the total number of the *ordres*: three × three = nine and three × nine = twenty-seven.[8] It is almost certainly also significant in the number of members in the Order of the Honey Bee. There are Masonic references amongst the titles of the *Pièces de Clavecin*,[9] and, importantly, the architecture of each *ordre* is carefully considered. This is not at first glance obvious, but an understanding of the titles Couperin gave the pieces not only helps the player to understand this elusive music but makes the organization of the *ordres* clear.

As we shall see (p. 103), the subject of the first piece of all, *L'Auguste*, could be either Louis-Auguste, Duc Du Maine, or the exiled James II of England, who was referred to as Augustus; this noble and serious allemande would be appropriate in either case.

7. Olivier Baumont, 'L'Ordre chez François Couperin'.

8. I am grateful to Penelope Cave for this observation.

9. See, for instance, *Les Abeilles* (*First Ordre*), *Les Baricades Mistérieuses* (*Sixth Ordre*), *La Visionaire, La Misterieuse*, and *Les Ombres Errantes* (*Twenty-fifth Ordre*).

But, given the associations of the last piece in the long *First Ordre*, *Les plaisirs de Saint Germain en Laÿe*, the likelihood is James II, demonstrating Couperin's sense of symmetry. This dark and oppressive piece reflects the sombre mood of James's court. The mention of pleasures in the title is typical of Couperin's irony (see p. 111).

One of the most deceptive titles is *La Sophie*, often but, as we shall see (p. 195), wrongly, thought to be a pretty girl. If the piece is played in a gently beguiling manner, there is little contrast with the nostalgic *Gavote* and the heart-breaking *L'Epineuse* which precede and follow it in the *Twenty-sixth Ordre*. A *sofi* was in fact a whirling dervish and the music expresses this perfectly. This interpretation affects the architecture of the whole *ordre*: we no longer have three consecutive pieces in a somewhat similar vein; we have two gentle pieces separated by a whirlwind. So the *Twenty-sixth Ordre* goes from the impressively spacious allemande, *La Convalescente*, to the little *Gavote*, then to *La Sophie*, followed by *L'Epineuse* and finally, the strong and dramatic *Pantomime*. The only *ordre* that does not have a similar sense of design is the *Twenty-fifth*, which the composer confessed, in his preface to *Book IV*, was not complete.

Even the apparently ramshackle *Second Ordre* (pp. 112–19) has a design. Most of the first part appears to be a suite of dances, but this is not perhaps as clear-cut as it might seem. There is a tendency to separate this *ordre* after the *Rigaudon*, on the argument that the character pieces begin here because all the following pieces have titles. But this is not very convincing, because the opening allemande also has a title (*La Laborieuse*); so does the sarabande (*La Prude*) and also the next piece, *L'Antonine*, which is not a dance at all. In the *First Ordre*, Couperin follows his dance suite with a set of character pieces, which he begins with the very impressive *Les Silvains*, and ends, as we have seen, with the balancing *Les plaisirs de Saint Germain en Laÿe.* A composer with Couperin's overall sense of architecture would surely never open the long set of character pieces in the *Second Ordre* with the insignificant *La Charoloise.* The more convincing shape is perhaps *Allemande, Courante, Courante, Sarabande,* and there a pause; Couperin's predecessors, including Purcell, ended some of their suites with a sarabande. Then the majestic *L'Antonine* precedes a new set of dances. If, as seems likely, *L'Antonine* is Anthony Hamilton, the aristocratic Jacobite exile, expert dancer, poet and habitué of the Duchesse Du Maine's entourage, then it is possible that these dances, *Gavotte, Menuet, Canaries, Passepied* and *Rigaudon,* were written for the Duchess's entertainments. Next comes the little piece *La Charoloise* (one of the Duchesse Du Maine's titles), followed by *La Diane* with its *Fanfare,* and it is surely with this obvious finale that the first part of the *ordre* ends. All the Duchess's friends were given mythical names and Diane was her cousin, the Duchesse de Nevers. In a similar way Couperin has a *Fanfare* at the end of the first group of pieces, under the general title of *La Triomphante,* in the *Tenth Ordre.* If on the other hand *La Charoloise* refers to the Duchess's niece, Louise-Anne de Bourbon, also Mademoiselle de Charolais, this suite could have been written for one of Monsieur le Duc's entertainments.

Having finished with the dance suite, Couperin embarks on a wonderfully varied set of character pieces, beginning with *La Terpsicore,* surely Élisabeth Jacquet de La Guerre, who is referred to as Terpsichore in the dedication of her harpsichord pieces; this impressive opening bears a certain resemblance to her *Chaconne in D major.* All the pieces in this *ordre,* as always with Couperin, are sharply contrasted. To take the last three: *La Flateuse* – Couperin did not like flatterers; then *La Voluptueüse,* marked *tendrement &c* – he did like sexy girls and this piece is absolutely sincere; and finally *Les Papillons*, not in its most obvious meaning, butterflies, because Couperin's pieces are about people: *papillons* here are diamond-headed hairpins that flashed as heads turned. This piece is hard as nails, sophisticatedly flirtatious, brilliant and heartless, a virtuosic conclusion to this mighty *ordre*.

In the *Eighth Ordre* the architecture is superb. It opens with the dramatic and declamatory *La Raphaéle*, followed by a quick Corellian *Allemande*, then two contrasted *Courantes* and a grand *Sarabande*, all in *goûts-réunis* style. Next a gentle *Gavotte*, a light-hearted *Rondeau* and a *Gigue*, all in the French style, and finally, you might think, the famous *Passacaille*. Couperin's great *Passacaille* is a theatrical piece, a perpetual tug-of-war between the *rondeau* and the *couplets*, a human pleading with a force as inevitable as the seasons, but it is still a dance and the cumulative excitement is tremendous.

This *ordre*, an exercise in the *goûts-réunis* style Couperin was so fond of, is full of angular Italian-style declamation, something he may have heard in Alessandro Scarlatti's cantata recitatives at Saint-Germain.[10] But is all this drama too overwhelming? Couperin's ever-present sense of proportion compels him to restore us to normality by ending this powerful *ordre* with one of the most beguiling of all his pieces, *La Morinéte*. But does its presence upset the architecture? Indeed it does. So Couperin pays tribute to Jean Baptiste Morin, who wrote the first *goûts-réunis* French cantatas, some of which had optional alleluya finales. For all the drama of the *ordre*, there is a detachment here; indeed some of the Italianate figures approach the parodies found in theatre music, hence Couperin's wish to bring us down to earth, to laugh at us gently, but only if we so wish.

10. Edward Corp, 'The exiled court'.

The other great passacaille, *L'Amphibie* in the *Twenty-fourth Ordre*, is a very different affair. The *ordre* opens with *Les Vieux Seigneurs*, a *sarabande grave*. But unlike the other sarabandes, which, with the notable exception of *La Prude*, are written in such a way that they sound magnificent whatever you do to them, simply because the harpsichord cannot help it, this one, even more than *La Prude*, is written in such a high register that it is positively prevented from sounding grand. This is a satirical portrait of obsequious courtiers, calculating every move, flattering those that matter. Its pendant, *Les Jeunes Seigneurs, Cy-devant les petits Maitres*, is, as the playwright Dufresny says, more sincere. The *petits Maitres* ('fops'), whose speech is 'high and low' like the music, may be disorganized, garrulous, unthinking, but they have their sublime moments.

We then get on to the fatal ladies with *Les Dars-homicides*, Cupid's fatal darts, a delightfully flirtatious piece, followed by *Les Guirlandes*, marked *amoureusement*, presumably the result of the darts. After this beautiful piece satire sets in again with *Les Brinborions*, immensely long, in four sections, ruthlessly sending up feminine vanities, and this is followed by a portrait of a society lady drooling over her lap-dog, *La Divine-Babiche ou les amours badins*, a marked contrast to *Les Guirlandes*.

A tiny vaudeville, *La Belle Javotte autre fois L'Infante*, separates this from *L'Amphibie*, which is the final piece in this case, unlike the *Eighth Ordre* with its unexpected coda. But the vaudeville is also amphibious because the tune has been used to portray both a girl of low rank and the Spanish Infanta. As we have seen (pp. 79–81), vaudeville tunes were used over and over again in completely different situations. So, the opening courtiers were two-faced, amphibious, the *petits-maîtres* were effeminate, amphibious, and in *L'Amphibie* we are back where we started: the circle is complete.

Alexander Pope, in his *Epistle to Dr. Arbuthnot* (1735), penned perhaps the most devastating portrait of the 'Amphibious thing' in his lines on Lord Hervey, a courtier he could not abide. Couperin could not abide hypocrisy and flattery; they rear their heads in many pieces. In *L'Amphibie* he joins Pope in portraying 'wit that can creep and pride that licks the dust'. To view this piece simply as a noble passacaille is to miss all the many subtleties within it. The composer has marked it *noblement*, another example of Couperin's irony, and in a sense it is noble. It is a piece in which you are never certain where you are, which was presumably the intention.

We have remarked (p. 17) on Couperin's obsessive attitude to his instructions being obeyed, as set out in the preface to *Book III* of his pieces. Nowhere is this more important than in *La Verneüil* (*Eighteenth Ordre*), where he has marked an appoggiatura in the opening (and subsequent) chords, a unique instance among his allemandes. There is a tendency for players to ignore this instruction, and so instead of the dramatic, declamatory entrance of the great tragic actor, we have just another allemande, whereas all Couperin's allemandes have their own individual character which relates to the rest of the *ordre*. *La Verneüil* is a startling contrast to the sophisticated charm of Verneuil's wife, *La Verneüilléte*, whose portrait follows his.

By now it may be becoming clear that in order to appreciate the architecture of the *ordres* it is essential to try and find out what 'subjects' Couperin had in his mind when he composed the pieces. If the significance of his reference to Morin's cantatas is not appreciated, the position of *La Morinéte* in the *Eighth Ordre* may be misunderstood. If the implications of amphibians in the eighteenth century is not realized, the subtleties of *L'Amphibie* and its relationship with the other pieces in the *Twenty-fourth Ordre* may be missed. Some knowledge of the patrons of the *divertissement* helps to clarify the design of the *Second Ordre* and to appreciate the humour of the *Sixth*. The fact that the Prince de Conti had a laugh like a donkey makes it clear that he is the subject of the radiant allemande that opens the *Sixteenth Ordre*, and consequently the irony of the next piece, *L'Himen-amour*, and how it relates to him and his marital situation, can be appreciated. The fallen morals of the Jacobins, the familiar name for the Dominican order of monks and nuns, account for *Les Culbutes Ixcxbxnxs* (*Jacobines*, not, as is sometimes thought, Jacobites), and so its position in the *Nineteenth Ordre*, a powerful sexy romp separating the innocent charm of *L'Artiste* from the beautiful portrait of the talented musician Mademoiselle de La Plante, *La Muse-Plantine*, is understood.

Many of the *ordres* have a unity. For instance the *Sixth* seems to be dominated by the Duchesse Du Maine, the *Thirteenth* by the Regent, Philippe d'Orléans, the *Fourteenth* by playful love, the *Seventeenth* by Forqueray, and the *Eighteenth* and *Twenty-third* by the theatre. The *Twenty-first* and the *Twenty-second* are about love affairs that go wrong, one regretful and the other comic. It seems there is a conscious plan in almost every *ordre* and always a strong contrast between adjacent pieces. If the Grand Lodge of France is right in its belief that Couperin was a Freemason, this may be the answer to the puzzle over his use of the word *ordre*, and a sign that all his *ordres* save one, the *Twenty-fifth*, have an architectural plan.

JC

Catalogue of movements of the
Pièces de Clavecin

book i (1713)

Premier Ordre

The architecture of this *ordre* is touched upon on pp. 95–6.

Allemande l'Auguste

There are two contenders for the honour of this serious and dignified opening allemande, Louis-Auguste, Duc Du Maine, and the exiled James II, who was often referred to as Augustus in royalist iconography. The Duc Du Maine was Louis XIV's favourite and illegitimate son by Madame de Montespan. Mademoiselle de Launay describes him:

> Monsieur Du Maine was a man of an enlightened understanding, ingenious and cultivated, possessed of all the usual accomplishments, especially knowledge of the world to an eminent degree, and of a noble and serious disposition. Religion perhaps rather than nature had endowed him with all the virtues and kept him faithful to his practice of them. He loved order, respected justice and never disregarded decorum. His tastes tended to solitude, study and work. Gifted with all that makes one amiable in society, he lent himself to it with great repugnancy. When there, however, he was gay, easy, obliging and ever equable. His conversation, unaffected and sprightly, was replete with charm, and of a slight and graceful turn; his anecdotes were amusing, his manners nobly familiar and polite, his air ingenuous. The secrets of his heart were not discoverable;

mistrust guarded the entrance, and few sentiments made the effort to escape.[1]

In view of the final piece in this *ordre*, *Les plaisirs de Saint Germain en Laÿe*, James II perhaps has the stronger claim.

Premiere Courante

A slow and seductive courante of the vocal type. These were sung with varied *reprises*. Varied *reprises* had amorous connotations and the fact that the performers understood the conventions of ornamentation implied an amorous understanding. This is illustrated in paintings by Watteau, notably *La Gamme d'amour* and *La Leçon d'amour*.[2] In the fourth *Concert Royal* Couperin marked this type of French courante to be played *galamment*, that is amorously.

Seconde Courante

Of the dance type, a contrast to the first. The courante was a grave and dignified dance in France and its tempo was the slowest of all French court dances. In *Les Nations* Couperin gives many helpful indications as to the character of the courantes. Those in *La Françoise* 'noblement' and 'un peu plus viste', in *L'Espagnole* 'noblement' and 'un peu plus vivement', in *L'Impériale* the second 'plus marqué', in *La Piémontoise* the second 'un peu plus gayement'.

Sarabande la Majestueuse

Louis XIV. A fitting tribute to the king who was obsessed with 'La Gloire' and who built the chateau of Versailles as the status symbol to end all status symbols.

1. Madame de Staal de Launay, *Memoirs*, II, p. 206.
2. A.-P. de Mirimonde, 'Les sujets musicaux chez Antoine Watteau', p. 267.

Gavotte

A contrast to the grandeur of *La Majestueuse*. D'Anglebert included two similar gavottes in his *Pièces de Clavecin*; they are
subtitled *Airs anciens* and marked *lentement*. In his preface he said
of them: 'These little Airs are of an extraordinary finesse and have
a noble simplicity that has always pleased everyone.' Blavet used a
gavotte as a slow movement.

> It is entirely inappropriate to find fault with singers of these little airs
> when they take certain liberties with the structure of the music in
> order to make them more tender. [...] They often slow down the
> tempo in order to give themselves time to add ornaments. [...] This
> can be observed most often in certain older Gavottes which demand a
> greater degree of expression and tenderness. [...] It is completely
> unfair to criticise this style of performing by saying the airs are not
> danceable as thousands of ignoramuses have done. [...] However,
> this observation applies only to certain Gavottes. [...] It is always
> necessary to maintain the metric proportions so as not to alter a
> Minuet or a Sarabande to such an extent that it becomes a song in
> free meter, such as is usually implied by the term *Air*.[3]

La Milordine, Gigue

This type of gigue was thought to have originated in England.
Presumably this one portrays an English milord from the exiled
Stuart court at Saint-Germain-en-Laye, with which Couperin was
associated. When Couperin's carefully marked fingering is observed this proud young man struts along in his new Parisian
finery, entirely befitting the description the architect Robert Adam
sent home to his mother from Paris: 'A most frenchified head of
hair, loaded with powder, ornaments his top, a complete suit of

3. Bénigne de Bacilly, *A Commentary upon the Art of Proper Singing, 1668*,
p. 48.

cut velvet of two colours, his body, a solitaire ribbon his neck, Brussels lace his breast & hands.'[4]

Menuet

This was the most elegant of French court dances, with complex step patterns, performed in a moderately slow tempo. It was the most popular dance in France at the time.

Les Silvains

In July 1702 the elite of the King's Musicians appeared as Sylvains (gods of the forest who guard the flocks) in a *divertissement* at Châtenay given in honour of the Duc Du Maine's two-year-old son, the Prince de Dombes (see p. 24). Malézieu, dressed as the *Sylvain de Châteney* (his adopted title), sang verses in honour of this august guest, who had been born in his house:

> Un prince issu du sang de mille rois
> A respiré chez moi pour la première fois.[5]

(A prince descended from the blood of a thousand kings drew his first breath in my dwelling.)

No one knows who wrote the music for the *divertissement*; it may have been by Couperin, since the words fit his tune.[6] This piece was evidently popular, since it was arranged for the lute by Robert de Visée and survives in a manuscript, begun in 1699 but continued until at least 1716, *Manuscrit Vaudry de Saizenay.*[7] Couperin has marked his piece *majestueusement*, as befits a prince. Much of it

---

4. John Fleming, *Robert Adam and his Circle*, p. 113.

5. Piépape, *A Princess of Strategy*, p. 47.

6. Cessac, 'La duchesse du Maine et la musique', p. 99.

7. Now in the Bibliothèque de la Ville, Besançon, ms. 279.152-279.153. I am grateful to Tim Crawford and David Ledbetter for information on this manuscript.

could be the accompaniment to a missing vocal line, so it is possible that both the keyboard and the lute versions are arrangements, as are many of the pieces in *Book I*. It is known that de Visée played in the later *divertissements*, so the likelihood is that he played in this one as well.[8]

Les Abeilles

Originally published in 1707 as *L'Abeille*, this may be a reference to the Duchesse Du Maine's own order of chivalry, the Order of the Honey Bee, whose motto was taken from Tasso: 'The bee is small but she makes big wounds.' The Duchess was also very small; she and her two sisters were known not as the Princesses of the Blood but as the Dolls of the Blood.[9] *Les Abeilles* is one of the shortest harpsichord pieces. The Duchess's secret order had thirty-nine members (see p. 93). A choir and orchestra provided cantatas at the initiation ceremonies. Some of Couperin's lost cantatas may have been written for these ceremonies. This piece is a contrast to the grandeur of *Les Silvains*.

The change from one bee to many bees in the title may have been caused by the fact that, when the Duchess's order was formed, she had not completed the decorations at Sceaux, in which, eventually, bees could be seen everywhere.

La Nanète

Perhaps Anne Bulkeley, second Duchess of Berwick, known as Nanette, who married the Duke in 1700. This may be a country dance, since her stepson, the Duke of Liria, said of his mother, the first Duchess: 'She was vivacious and loved dancing. She never missed a festivity, and it was she who introduced the fashion for

8. Cessac, 'Un portrait musical de la duchesse du Maine', p. 38.
9. Piépape, *A Princess of Strategy*, p. 11.

English country dances to the court of France.'[10] This claim is not strictly true, as they seem to have reached France with Charles II during his exile, but it is possible that the first Duchess of Berwick revived and popularized them. The Duke of Berwick was an illegitimate son of James II and resident in France. His second wife may also have been a keen dancer of the *contredanse anglaise*; she was reported at Marly dancing country dances in 1711.[11] There was also a Mademoiselle Nanette in the entourage of the Duchesse Du Maine.[12]

Les Sentimens, Sarabande
An amorous sarabande.

La Pastorelle
Originally published as a vocal piece. Marked *naivement*, it is a contrast to the pieces that frame it. Presumably Couperin put this tiny piece in for just that reason.

Les Nonètes
The young nuns, first the *blondes* and then the *brunettes*. Perhaps the piece refers to the Loyson sisters (see p. 50, *Les Juméles, Twelfth Ordre*, and *Les Chérubins ou L'aimable Lazure, Twentieth Ordre*) for whom Regnard wrote his *Chanson pour Mlles. Loyson* in 1702:

> Par la Doguine
> Qu'un autre se laisse enflammer:
> Si je n'avois point vu Tontine
> Je pourrois me laisser charmer
> Par la Doguine.

10. Sir Charles Petrie, *The Duke of Berwick and his Son*, p. 101.
11. Corp, 'Les courtisans français', p. 60, n. 73.
12. Madame de Staal de Launay, *Memoirs*, I, p. 125.

> Ou brune ou blonde,
> Tontine charme également;
> Et, pour contenter tout le monde,
> Elle est alternativement
> Ou brune ou blonde.

(Let someone else be smitten by Doguine; if I had not seen Tontine, I could have let myself be charmed by Doguine. Whether she be brunette or blonde, Tontine is equally charming; and, to keep everyone happy, she is alternatively brunette or blonde.)

Furetière reveals that a *nonnette* is a marsh-tit as well as a nun. When used in the burlesque style (a style often indicated by Couperin; see for example *Le Gaillard-Boiteux, Eighteenth Ordre*) it means that these young ladies 'font en amour tous les tours les plus fins. Dans un couvent de Nonnes frequentoit un jouvenceau friand de ces oiseaux, pas une n'est qui montre en ce dessin de la froideur, soit Nonne, soit Nonnette' (they 'are up to all the finest tricks of love. A young man who frequented a convent of these birds did not find one who greeted his designs with coldness, whether nun or nonnette'). Furetière also says: 'Les beautés blondes durent moins que les beautés brunes, elles sont moins vives et moins animées' ('Blonde beauties wear less well than brunettes, they are less lively and less fun'). These seductive and flirtatious nuns are a contrast to the simplicity of *La Pastorelle*. A dotted compound rhythm is often used by Couperin in his portraits of women of dubious morals (see *La Babet, Second Ordre*, and *La Fringante, Tenth Ordre*). It signified horse-riding; the explanation is found in his vocal canon *La Femme entre deux Draps* (see p. 33), where the words refer to being unsaddled and thrown by lively women.

La Bourbonnoise, Gavotte

Louise-Françoise, Duchesse de Bourbon, wife of Monsieur le Duc, a pupil of Couperin. A good dancer, this mischievous and popular sister of the Duc Du Maine once borrowed a pipe from the guardroom and filled the royal apartment with smoke. She was threatened with banishment to the country. She could drink any woman and most men under the table and was always in a good temper. Her comic and often indecent verses were genuinely amusing except to the victims. Reproached with having a gizzard instead of a heart, she was nonetheless the object of the constant affection of the Prince de Conti (see *Sixteenth Ordre*).[13]

The subject could also be her daughter, Louise-Élisabeth de Bourbon, a pupil of Couperin (see p. 21).

La Manon

Daughter of the playwright Florent Dancourt, a *comédienne* who made her début in 1699. Marked *vivement*; Furetière: 'Avec ardeur, avec vigueur, sans relache' ('With ardour, with energy, without respite').

L'Enchanteresse

Also the title of a painting by Watteau, in which a young man plays the guitar to two girls on the banks of a river, so this is a male enchanter, in contrast to the next piece. In the lute/guitar register, with its classic portrayal of musical water in the final couplet, this piece could have inspired the title of the painting. There was a proverb: 'L'art enchanteur du luth aide à obtenir la faveur des belles' ('The charm of the lute helps to obtain the favour of beautiful ladies').[14]

---

13. W. H. Lewis, *The Sunset of the Splendid Century*, p. 90.
14. Mirimonde, 'Les sujets musicaux chez Antoine Watteau', p. 271.

La Fleurie ou La tendre Nanette

Probably the Dauphin's daughter by the actress La Raisin (see p. 36 and *La Tendre Fanchon, Fifth Ordre*), 'lovely as an angel', whom he called Mademoiselle de Fleury after a village in the park at Meudon.[15] Anne Louise de Fleury was brought up and given a dowry by the Dowager Princesse de Conti (see pp. 36–7), a pupil of Couperin and dedicatee of D'Anglebert's *Pièces de Clavecin*. She married Anne Errard, Marquis d'Avaugour.

Les plaisirs de Saint Germain en Laÿe

Couperin had a house at Saint-Germain from 1710 to 1716, presumably to be near his pupils at the exiled Stuart court and to enable him to take part in the musical activities there, which had increased since the death of James II in 1701. The title of this fine, but dark and somewhat oppressive piece could be ironic. The atmosphere created by the intense piety of Mary of Modena and her guilt-ridden husband in his hair shirt, both frequently taking refuge in the respective convents of Chaillot and La Trappe, must at times have been stifling, particularly to the younger members of the court. The Queen even questioned the advisability of her children being allowed to go to the Opéra.[16] Her great friend Madame de Maintenon had no objection to the music of the opera, only to the words, in which, she said, 'one hears nothing but maxims absolutely opposed to the Gospel and Christianity'.[17]

15. *Letters from Liselotte*, p. 149, 9 May 1711.
16. Corp, 'The exiled court', p. 223.
17. Cuthbert Girdlestone, *Jean-Philippe Rameau*, p. 528.

Second Ordre

The architecture of this *ordre* is discussed on pp. 96–8.

Allemande La Laborieuse

Louis Le Laboureur was a man who published, in 1667, a famous book on *Les Avantages de la langue françoise sur la langue latine*. His name means 'ploughman', but it is characteristic of Couperin to use feminine adjectival forms in his titles, particularly when he begins with the name of a dance form, and he must have been pleased with the fact that the related adjective here is both less specific in its application and more complimentary, for, when applied to people, *laborieux* meant 'hardworking'. This allemande is written in the Italian contrapuntal style but civilized by French ornamentation and performance style.[18] It is clear from *L'Art de toucher le clavecin* that Couperin thought the French had the edge on the Italians, though he admitted that there were faults in the way they wrote their music which, he said, corresponded to the way in which they wrote their language: 'The fact is we write it down differently from the way in which we play it.' In what is, presumably, a reference to Le Laboureur's book, Couperin instructs that the semiquavers are to be played *un tant-soit-peu pointées* ('ever so slightly dotted').

> Given two notes of equal length, one of them is interpreted as being dotted while the other is not. [...] It is necessary to interpret this dotted rhythm as delicately and subtly as possible so that it does not seem overdone. This technique must especially be utilised in specific places which would seem to demand this style of performance, and conversely, it must be assiduously avoided in other places.[19]

18. For a somewhat different view of this allemande see David Ledbetter, '*Les goûts réunis* and the music of J. S. Bach', p. 69.
19. Bacilly, *A Commentary upon the Art of Proper Singing*, p. 118.

Premiere Courante
Dance type (see *First Ordre, Seconde Courante,* p. 104).

Seconde Courante
Vocal type (see *First Ordre, Premiere Courante,* p. 104).

Sarabande la Prude
Madame de Maintenon, pendant to *La Majestueuse* (*First Ordre*).
Written in a high register like *Les Vieux Seigneurs* (*Twenty-fourth Ordre*), majesty becomes impossible; both are satirical sarabandes.

L'Antonine
Probably Anthony Hamilton, a Jacobite exile who lived at Saint-Germain. An accomplished dancer, he was a brilliant visitor to the Duchesse Du Maine's chateau of Sceaux. Known as Comte Antoine Hamilton, he was a brave field-marshal, a poet and a writer of romantic fiction, his best-known work being the *Mémoires de la vie du comte de Gramont,* in which he relates the exploits of his brother-in-law. In his poems he celebrated the beauties of the court at Saint-Germain. *L'Antonine* is a grand and outgoing piece, written with great resonance in mind; it makes *La Prude* sound petty by comparison. It is possible that this and the pieces that follow it, up to and including *La Diane,* with its *Fanfare,* were originally written for *divertissements* at Châtenay or for Monsieur le Duc. It is also possible that the dances were written for the far more modest entertainments held after the death of James II at Saint-Germain, which may have been inspired by those of the Duchess.

Gavotte
See *First Ordre,* p. 105.

Menuet
See *First Ordre,* p. 106.

Canaries, Double des Canaries
A dance that came to France from Spain. It had come from the Canary Islands and was described by Covarrubias Horozco in his *Tesoro de la lengua castellana o española* of 1611 as a type of *saltarelo grazioso.* The saltarello was a fairly quick Italian dance. Later the canaries became similar to a gigue but Couperin's is the earlier type. In France it was often used as a stage dance.

Passe-pied
A French court dance that was a faster version of the minuet. It too was often a stage dance.

Rigaudon
Another French court dance that had its heyday at the end of the seventeenth century and on into the eighteenth, when it was often used as a stage dance. As a social dance it was often one of the many kinds of contredanse.

La Charoloise
One of the titles of the Duchesse Du Maine, perhaps another tiny piece referring to her minute size (see *Les Abeilles, First Ordre*). Or possibly the Duchess's niece, daughter of Monsieur le Duc, Louise-Anne de Bourbon, also Mademoiselle de Charolais. She was a pupil of Couperin (see p. 21).

La Diane, Fanfare pour la Suitte de la Diane
The goddess Diana, the huntress. The Duchesse Du Maine's friends had mythical names; Diana was her cousin, the Duchesse

de Nevers.[20] Probably either a reference to, or part of, a
divertissement (see *L'Antonine*).

La Terpsicore

The similarity between this piece and Élisabeth Jacquet de La
Guerre's *Chaconne in D major*, and the fact that she was referred to
as Terpsichore in the dedication of her harpsichord pieces, suggest
that she is the subject.[21]

La Florentine

Because the other members of his family appear (in the *First*,
Second and *Sixteenth Ordres*), this piece may refer to Florent
Dancourt, the actor and playwright. The charm of the piece could
fit his description by Titon Du Tillet:

> Les agrémens de sa conversation et sa politesse le faisoient rechercher
> par tout ce qu'il y avoit de plus grand à la court et à la ville; et les
> personnes plus considerables se faisoient un plaisir de l'avoir chez eux
> et de l'aller voir chez lui. La facilité qu'il avoit à parler et une
> éloquence naturelle qui animoit tous ses discours, lui avoit fait déferer
> par ses camarades l'honneur de porter la parole dans toutes les
> occasions particulières, et le public l'écoutait toujours avec
> applaudissement.[22]

> (A civilized and charming man, his company was sought by the most
> important people of the court and the city. The ease with which he
> spoke and the natural eloquence that enlivened all his speeches have
> made his comrades bestow on him the honour of speaking on all
> special occasions, and the public always cheers him.)

He was later criticized for having portrayed only bad morals in his
comedies. The same thing could be said of Couperin. Dancourt's

---

20. Piépape, *A Princess of Strategy*, p. 70.
21. I am grateful to Francis Monkman for pointing this out to me.
22. Titon Du Tillet, *Le Parnasse françois*, p. 607.

play *Les Trois Cousines* is thought to be the inspiration for Watteau's painting *L'Embarquement pour Cithère*.

This piece is marked by Couperin to be played *d'une légéreté tendre*. Furetière's explanation of the meaning of *tendre* fits Dancourt: 'Il a l'âme tendre qui s'émeut facilement de compassion pour les misères de son prochain. Il aime ses amis d'une amitié tendre' ('He who has a sensitive spirit is easily touched with compassion for the troubles of his neighbour. He loves his friends with a tender affection').

Another candidate is a dancer called La Florence, a mistress of the future regent Philippe d'Orléans, Duc de Chartres, whom he removed from the Opéra and installed in a smart house in Paris in 1697 (see p. 36).[23] One of many satirical verses on the subject relates how, on the arrival of a troupe from the Opéra:

> Monsieur le duc de Chartres,
> Comme prince du sang,
> Faisoit le diable à quatre
> Pour avoir le devant;
> Il tenoit par la main
> La Charmante Florence.[24]

(The Duc de Chartres, as a royal prince, kicked up a shindy to be in front; he held the charming Florence by the hand.)

La Garnier

The organist Gabriel Garnier, who was said to play Couperin's music better than the composer himself.

La Babet

Élisabeth Danneret, known as Babet la Chanteuse, wife of the Arlequin Evaristo Gherardi (see *Twenty-third Ordre*). She was

23. *Letters from Liselotte*, p. 76.
24. *Recueil*, dit de Maurepas, *Pièces Libres, Chansons, Épigrammes*, II, p. 319.

pretty, had a very pleasant voice and was a sensational success in every role she undertook. After her husband's death she joined the Royal Academy of Music. Presumably she lived up to the dubious reputation of its members (see *La Tendre Fanchon*, *Fifth Ordre*) because Couperin used a dotted 6/8 rhythm to imply horse-riding (see *Les Nonètes*, *First Ordre*, and *La Fringante*, *Tenth Ordre*), which in its turn implied dubious morals (see the canon *La Femme entre deux Draps* on p. 33). Another possibility is the dancer Élisabeth Dufort, also known as Babet, a soloist at the Opéra. Marked *nonchalammant*, this separates two intense pieces.

Les Idées Heureuses

Fantasies. Couperin holds this piece in his portrait by Bouys.

La Mimi

Mimi, actress daughter of Florent Dancourt; probably the subject of Watteau's *La Finette*, because she played La Finette, a sly sou-brette role, in several of her father's plays and had a great success. Her daughter married Rameau's patron La Poupelinière.

La Diligente

A charming and witty portrait of someone practising. A genuine and straightforward piece in contrast to the previous and the next.

La Flateuse

A musical portrayal of a flatterer, based perhaps on real life, perhaps on a scene from a play like the following from Boisfran's *Arlequin misanthrope*:

> Mr. de la Cabriole Maistre à Danser, Mr. de Geresol Maistre à
>   chanter (Ils font plusieurs reverences).
> ARLEQUIN: Quelle reverence! Encore … Ouf. Je n'y sçaurois durer.
> M. DE GERESOL: Je ne sçay, Monsieur, si vous nous connoissez.
> ARLEQUIN: Non, & je n'en ay mesme aucune envie.
> M. DE GERESOL: Nous venons vous assurer de nos respects.

M. DE LA CABRIOLE: Nous n'avons pas voulu manquer cette occasion
de vous faire la reverance.
ARLEQUIN: En voila déja plus de quinze de faites.[25]

(M. de La Cabriole Dancing Master, M. de Geresol Singing Master
(They make several bows).
HARLEQUIN: What bowing! Again … Ouf. I can't bear it.
M. DE GERESOL: I don't know, Sir, if you know who we are.
HARLEQUIN: No, and I don't want to.
M. DE GERESOL: We come to assure you of our respect.
M. DE LA CABRIOLE: We didn't want to miss this occasion of making
you a bow.
HARLEQUIN: Well, you've already made more than fifteen.)

Couperin clearly had little use for flatterers, so the marking
affectueusement (affectionately) is puzzling, as it is with several
other pieces; there are many occasions when it appears to be ironic.
Furetière: 'Les Princes n'ont point de plus dangereux ennemis que
les flateurs' ('Princes have no more dangerous enemies than
flatterers'). However, Furetière also says that *affectueux* can be used
'dans les matières de pieté, pour marquer ce qui vient du cœur' ('in
matters of piety, to show what comes from the heart'). It is
possible that Couperin twisted the meaning to give it a Tartuffe-
like hypocritical connotation.

La Voluptueüse

Marked *tendrement, &c.* A genuine compliment to a sexy girl, in
contrast to the previous piece.

Les Papillons

These *papillons* are no more real butterflies than Couperin's
rossignol is a real bird (see *Fourteenth Ordre*) or his *moucheron* a real

---

25. Boisfran, *Arlequin misanthrope*, in Gherardi, *Le Théâtre italien*, VI, p. 556.

gnat (see *Sixth Ordre*). A character in Boursault's play *Les Mots à la mode* explains:

> Les papillons ce sont les diamans du bout de nos poinçons, qui, remuant toujours et jettant mille flammes, paroissent voltiger dans les cheveux des dames.[26]

> (Papillons are the diamonds at the ends of pins, which, shaking and throwing out a thousand flames, appear to fly about in our hair.)

Flirtatious and light-hearted in contrast to *La Voluptueüse*. *Papillon* also means a flirt.

Troisième Ordre

La Ténébreuse, Allemande

Furetière: 'Sombre, obscur, melancolique' ('Sombre, dark, melancholic'). The first six sombre pieces of the *ordre* could refer, as *La Favorite* appears to, to the gloom that had descended on the court or to a *divertissement* (see p. 26). At the beginning of the eighteenth century France was ruined by the War of the Spanish Succession. The courtiers were all in financial difficulties and the King's health was failing. Famine spread throughout France.

It has been suggested that this allemande could be a *tombeau*. Music engraving was slow and expensive, but if there had been time between the death of Couperin's pupil, the young Dauphin, in February 1712 and the publication of *Book I* in May 1713, this could be the case. Or indeed this powerful piece could reflect the intense grief of the court after the deaths of all Louis XIV's young relatives. The Grand Dauphin had died from smallpox the previous year and an outbreak of measles caused the deaths of his

26. Boursault, *Les Mots à la mode*, quoted in Franklin, *La Vie privée*, XV, *Les Magasins de Nouveauté*, I, p. 239.

son, the young Dauphine and their eldest son. Only their younger son, the future Louis XV, survived.

But perhaps this obvious subject is unlikely since Couperin said in his preface to *Book I* that work on this volume had been going on for over a year. Another possible candidate is James II, who had died in 1701. But perhaps the most likely subject of all was the Prince de Conti, who died in 1709. He was mourned by people of all ranks, and Couperin would certainly have been amongst them.

Premiere Courante
This gentle, vocal courante seems to awake from the darkness of the allemande.

Seconde Courante
Once more the courantes are contrasted, the second being more dramatic.

La Lugubre, Sarabande
Furetière: 'Il y a des musiques des tons lugubres. Triste, melancolique, funebre' ('Some music is lugubrious in tone. Sad, melancholic, funereal'). (See p. 26.)

Gavotte
See *First Ordre*, p. 105.

Menuet
See *First Ordre*, p. 106.

Les Pélerines:
   La Marche
   La Caristade
   Le Remerciement
Originally a vocal piece, published in 1712. The pilgrims are pilgrims of love bound for the Island of Cythera. In three sections,

the first being a march to the Temple of Love, the second the giving of alms, and the third the thanksgiving:

La Marche

Au Temple de l'Amour
Pellerines de Cythère,
Nous allons d'un cœur sincère
Nous offrir à notre tour;
Les Ris, les Jeux, les Amours
Sont du voyage,
Les doux soupirs,
Les tendres désirs
Sont le but de ce pélerinage,
Le prix en est les Plaisirs.

(Pilgrims of Cythera, we offer ourselves at the temple of love with sincere hearts. The voyage is one of laughter, games and love; sweet sighs, tender desires are the purpose of this pilgrimage, the prize is pleasure.)

La Caristade

Au nom charmant de ces vives flâmes
Qui causent aux âmes
Tant de douceurs,
Soyez touchés de nos langueurs;
On lit dans nos yeux le besoin de nos cœurs.

(In the enchanting name of these passionate flames which cause our souls so much sweetness, be moved by our sighs; you read in our eyes the desires of our hearts.)

Le Remerciement

Que désormais des biens durables
A jamais comblent vos souhaits!
Vos tendres soins, vos dons secourables
Nous soulagent dans ce jour.
Puisse l'Amour
Vous rendre en retour
Encore plus charitables!

(Hereafter may lasting blessings fulfil your wishes! Your tender care, your willing gifts comfort us this day. May love make you, in return, even more charitable!)

These words appear on an engraving of 1725 which shows a *Pélerine pour le Divertissement du Voyage à Cithère.*[27] Perhaps this is a sure indication that Couperin did in fact write music for *divertissements.* It makes a sharp contrast to the seriousness of the previous pieces.

Les Laurentines

The Laurent family had their fingers in many pies for several generations: one was the *concierge* of the Comédie Française, another was a dancer and another a singer.[28] One did walk-on parts for Molière: he makes an appearance as Tartuffe's valet where he has his own name. 'Laurent' is in fact the first word spoken by Tartuffe when he makes his long-awaited entrance.[29] François Laurent opened a famous literary café in 1690. To judge by the portrait that emerges if Couperin's copious markings are observed 'to the letter' (as he insisted in his preface to *Book III*), it seems likely that he was either following the satirists in sending up the pretensions and affectations of the *littérateurs* who gathered at the Café Laurent[30] or he was satirizing the family itself. The café was in the Rue Dauphine and still exists. It was a favourite with Jean-Baptiste Rousseau and Voltaire, who drank *Eau de Café* there, and later became a haunt for François Mauriac, Jean-Paul Sartre, Boris Vian, Juliette Gréco and Brigitte Bardot. Rousseau's misfortunes (he was prosecuted for defamation of character) began with a

27. Illustrated in Wilfrid Mellers, *François Couperin and the French Classical Tradition*, p. 393.
28. Émile Campardon, *Les Comédiens du Roi de la Troupe Française*, p. 238.
29. *Le Tartuffe*, III, ii.
30. Maurepas, *Recueil*, II, p. 131, III, p. 91.

squabble at the Café Laurent, where he indulged in lampoons on his companions.

L'Espagnolète

A dance in which Manon Dancourt excelled. It was performed with castanets. Louis XIV's Spanish queen brought many Spanish dances to France. Perhaps a reference to more cheerful days at court. An *espagnolette* is also a window latch, the turning of which Couperin imitates in the turns on the second quaver of the opening phrase, and subsequently.[31]

Les Regrets

If this piece is somewhat satirical, as *languissamment* often implied, it could be pining for times gone by when life at the court, and in France generally, was happier. But if it is heartfelt it could refer to the death of the Prince de Conti (see *La Ténébreuse* above).

Les Matelotes Provençales

A dance that spread northwards from Provence in the eighteenth century. There were two versions, one slow and graceful and the other quick and springing.

La Favorite, Chaconne à deux tems

Possibly a reference to the economies at the court during the War of the Spanish Succession. In 1702 Madame de Maintenon insisted on austerity of dress. Ribbons, lace, embroideries etc. all disappeared at Versailles, smaller hats replaced the large plumed ones, silk stockings were replaced by cotton, the wearing of gold and silver ornaments was regulated. Habits were brown or amaranth. The only feature permitted was a long, broad ribbon, the *chaconne*.

31. Wilfrid Mellers, *François Couperin and the French Classical Tradition*, p. 394.

Françoise D'Aubigné, Marquise de Maintenon, as St Frances of Rome:
engraving by Étienne Ficquet (1759) after Pierre Mignard (1694)

La Favorite has two beats in the bar as opposed to the normal three, an economy indeed. The *favorite* was Madame de Maintenon herself, no one at that time knowing that she had married the King. Rousseau says in his dictionary that there used to be such a chaconne, but no longer[32]; it is possible that Couperin's was the first. The fourth *couplet* may portray the bored yawns of the courtiers, all impatient to be off to a *divertissement* for the final piece in the *ordre*.

La Lutine

A *lutin* was a lewd sprite that figured in plays and *divertissements*:

> Moi? Je suis le Lutin des nouvelles Folies,
> Chantons, rions, dansons, tâchons de vivre encore,
> Voyez mes grands cheveux faits de lumière et d'or!
> Et mes yeux de tisons d'enfer! Voyez mes lèvres
> Où l'amour et la lyre ont mis toutes leurs fièvres!
> Mes joyaux! Mes habits où ruissellent de fleurs!
> Pleurez-vous, cher monsieur? Je viens sécher les pleurs!
> Écoutez mes chansons de danseuse bohème!
> Et surtout, aimez-moi d'abord, je veux qu'on m'aime!
> Laissez-moi folâtrer, bacchante, avec mes sœurs,
> Et je vous verserai ce vin, cher aux penseurs
> Saintement couronnés de raisins et de lierre,
> Dont s'enivrait Le Sage et que goûtait Molière.[33]

(Me? I am the lutin of the new follies, let us sing, laugh, dance, let us try to live again, look at my long hair made of light and gold! And my hell-hounds' eyes! Look at my lips where love and music have placed all their passions! My jewels! My clothes streaming with flowers! Are you crying, dear sir? I will dry your tears. Listen to my songs of a gipsy dancer! Above all, love me, I want you to love me! Let me frolic like a bacchante with my sisters, and I will pour the

32. Jean-Jacques Rousseau, *Dictionnaire de musique*.
33. J. Baumgarten, *La France qui rit*, p. 90.

wine, dear to the philosophers crowned with sacred vines and ivy, of which Molière tasted and which intoxicated Lesage.)

At one of the *Grandes Nuits* sleep was chased from the chateau by the *Lutin de Sceaux*. With Couperin's sense of symmetry it is tempting to wonder whether the first and last pieces in this *ordre* refer to an earlier *divertissement* on the same subject. A sharp contrast to the pious gloom of *La Favorite*. (See p. 26.)

Quatrième Ordre

La Marche des Gris-vêtus

A drinking song in honour of the famous regiment with grey uniforms, the words of which go:

> Des gris-vêtus chantons la Gloire,
> Chantons leurs vertus quand il faut boire
> Et faisons l'honneur à leur vigueur.

(Let us sing the glory of the Grey Coats, let us sing their virtues when we drink, and pay respect to their strength.)

Les Baccanales:

> *Enjoüemens Bachiques*
> *Tendresses Bachiques*
> *Fureurs Bachiques*

In this suite within a suite, dedicated to the pleasures of Bacchus, a tipsy dance is followed by amorous advances which give way to wild abandon. Furetière: 'On appelloit la fête de Bacchanales, Orgies du mot Grec orgé, qui signifie fureur' ('Bacchanales were called orgies from the Greek word *orgy*, which means fury'). This is typical of *divertissements* at Châtenay and Sceaux.

La Pateline

Maistre Pierre Pathelin was an anonymous fifteenth-century farce, adapted in 1706 by Brueys and Palaprat. Pathelin was an out-of-work, impecunious advocate, who wheedled goods out of unsuspecting tradesmen by piling one insincere flattery on top of another. By the time the play was revived and Couperin wrote this piece *patelin* had entered the vocabulary. Furetière: 'Homme adroit, fourbe, qui trompe les hommes, souple et artificieux qui par ses manières flateuses et insinuantes fait venir les autres à ses fins. Ce nom vient d'un homme Patelin Avocat' ('An artful man, a swindler, who takes people in, supple and cunning, who by his flattering and insinuating manners uses others for his ends. The name comes from a man, Patelin Avocat'). It was used of priests like Tartuffe:

> Pathelin
> Adroit hipocrite,
> Courtisan fin,
> Rusé catamite,
> Sous les juppes
> Que tu dupes,
> Caches toy
> Prelet sans foy.[34]

(Clever hypocrite, subtle courtier, deceitful catamite, hide yourself under the skirts that you dupe, prelate without faith.)

Le Réveil-matin

The alarm clock. Contemporary accounts abound in descriptions of people unable to get out of bed the morning after the night before (see p. 26).

34. Satirical poem, British Library, King's MSS, 337, f. 51.

Cinquième Ordre

La Logiviére, Allemande

An example of Couperin's habit of punning, this has to be Jean Antoine Logi, or Losy (but pronounced 'Logy'), the Bohemian count who was a keen and expert lutenist and composer, remembered nowadays for his beautiful *Tombeau* written by Sylvius Leopold Weiss. His allemande is written in the *style brisé* of the lute. The figuration in the second half betrays the influence of Bohemian lute style, typical of Logi but not normal for Couperin. Inspection of Logi's music might reveal references in this piece, and possibly in the two courantes that follow it. It is likely that Logi, who held an Imperial post, visited Paris on an official mission from the Austrian Emperor; his music reveals an intimate knowledge of French lute style. The *Manuscrit Vaudry de Saizenay* (see *Les Silvains, First Ordre*) includes a piece by him, the *Rondeau du Comte de Logis*, which immediately provides a link between Couperin, de Visée and Logi. Logi's title was Comte de Losinthal (German *Thal* means 'valley'), so, had Couperin translated the name literally, he might have called the piece *Logival* (French *val* means a steep, narrow valley). But perhaps he thought a river (French *rivière*) sounded better than a valley (see *La Létiville, Sixteenth Ordre*). There is in fact a river Linth in Switzerland where the title comes from; it runs down a steep, narrow valley, the Linthal. Logi's (Losi's) father, who was Swiss, simply included his name, arriving at 'Losinthal'. Couperin was by no means alone in playing with names.[35]

35. I am grateful to Tim Crawford, Elizabeth Kenny and Benjamin Narvy for help with this entry.

Perhaps the style of this allemande is that of the somewhat unmeasured allemandes so common in seventeenth-century lute and harpsichord music.

Première Courante
The vocal type (see *First Ordre*, p. 104).

Seconde Courante
A dance (see *First Ordre*, p. 104).

Sarabande la Dangereuse
Furetière: 'Les plaisirs sont les amusemens dangéreux. [...] Un plaisir indiscret est toujours dangéreux. [...] Vos yeux scavent lancer de trop dangéreux traits. [...] J'approuve le dessein que vous avez fait de vous desabuser de la fortune, et de la quitter comme une maitresse dangereuse' ('Pleasures are dangerous amusements. [...] An indiscreet pleasure is always dangerous. [...] Your eyes throw very dangerous darts. [...] I approve of the plan you have made to disabuse yourself of fortune, and to leave it like a dangerous mistress'). When applied to women in medieval and courtly French, *dangereuse* could mean haughty.[36]

Gigue
Similar gigues in Couperin's chamber music are marked *d'une légéreté modérée*.

La Tendre Fanchon
One of the most beautiful young ladies of her time, Françoise Moreau, known as Fanchon, was a singer like her sister Louison (Louise), who figures in Couperin's vocal canon *Les Trois Vestales Champêtres et Les Trois Poliçons* (see the *Sixteenth Ordre*). For twenty years Fanchon was the mistress of Philippe de Vendôme,

36. I am grateful to Brian Binding for this meaning.

Grand Prieur de France, but as she was not faithful the relationship was 'not without its clouds'.[37] They appear in a Noel of 1696:

> Le grand prieur s'avance,
> Suivi de sa Fanchon,
> Faisant la révérance,
> Dit au petit poupon,
> Avecque La Moreau,
> Je connois mon offense,
> J'ai péché tout de bon, don, don,
> Mais avec celle là la, la,
> J'en fais la pénitence.[38]

(The Grand Prieur advances, followed by his Fanchon; making his bow he says to the little baby [the Christ Child], I know my offence, I have sinned seriously with La Moreau, but with her I do my penance.)

When Fanchon played opposite Gabriel-Vincent Thévenard (see *La Gabriéle, Tenth Ordre*) she acted so well that she excited the jealousy of her lover. There are many stories about her, and she figures in Couperin's other vocal canon, *La Femme entre deux Draps* (Woman between two Sheets; see p. 33). Both sisters were members of the Royal Academy of Music, the Opéra, which had a bad name:

> Ce beau lieu fournit de belles
> À tous les gens d'à présent;
> Des Matins pour l'argent,
> La Moreau pour les dentelles,
> La Grand Diart pour son pain
> La Rochois le fait pour rien.[39]

---

37. Le Brisoys Desnoiresterres, *Cours galantes*, III, p. 154.

38. Maurepas, *Recueil*, II, p. 291.

39. Georges Mongrédien, *Daily Life in the French Theatre*, p. 206.

(This wonderful place provides beauties for everyone today; Des Matins for money, La Moreau for lace, La Grande Diart for her bread and La Rochois does it for nothing.)

A less likely candidate is Françoise Pitel de Longchamp, known as Fanchon Longchamps (see p. 37).

La Badine

Playful love. Furetière: 'Il n'y a rien plus agréable qu'un amour badin' ('There is nothing more pleasant than playful love'). One of Watteau's paintings was called *Les Amours badins*. A *badine* is also 'une canne légère, souple et pliante' ('a light stick, supple and pliant') used by young people and great noblemen, and by women for their morning walk.[40]

La Bandoline

Bandoline was a hair lacquer, made from the sticky juice of quinces. In 1713, the year in which *Book I* was published, the Duchess of Shrewsbury, wife of the English ambassador, wondered at the ladies' hairdressing in Paris. Saint Simon tells us: 'She pronounced it to be perfectly ridiculous, as indeed it was', he agrees, 'for they wore erections of wire, ribbons and false hair, supplemented with all manner of gewgaws, rising to a height of more than two feet. When they moved the entire edifice trembled and the discomfort was extreme.'[41] Madame de Maintenon wrote of the Duchesse Du Maine in 1692: 'Her headdress weighs more than she does.'[42] Louis XIV could not bear these *coiffures*, which started in the late 1680s. 'The *coiffures* grow taller and taller every day. The King told us at dinner today that a fellow by the name of Allart, who used to do people's hair here, has dressed all the ladies

40. Franklin, *La Vie privée*, XXII, *Les Magasins*, IV, p. 313.

41. *Saint Simon*, II, p. 284.

42. Piépape, *A Princess of Strategy*, p. 26.

of London so tall that they can't get into their sedan-chairs, and have been obliged to have them heightened in order to follow the French fashion.'[43] The Duchess of Shrewsbury changed it all. The King complained: 'I admit I am piqued when I see that with all my royal authority, I have inveighed against these ridiculously high coiffures, but not a single person had the least desire to lower them for me. Along comes someone completely unknown, a ragamuffin from England, with a small, low coiffure: all at once the princesses go from one extreme to the other.'[44]

The marking *légèrement* shows that the piece is meant as a joke. Furetière said of *léger* that it 'se dit figurement de ce qui est frivole' ('is used figuratively of what is frivolous'). With its legato right hand and its staggering octaves in the left this is a brilliant caricature.

La Flore

Spring. She often appeared in *divertissements*. In 1700 the Duchesse de Bourgogne's circle performed a masquerade entitled *La Flore*.[45] Alternatively Furetière gives a more likely meaning: 'Une fille qui ayant gagné beaucoup de bien par les débauches, institue les jeux floraux' ('A girl who, having gained great benefit from debauch, sponsors poetry competitions'). The Académie des Jeux Floraux was a literary society derived from Roman fêtes in honour of the goddess Flora. The members of the Academy rewarded the authors of the best poems with gold flowers.

A voluptuous piece in contrast to *La Bandoline*.

43. *Letters from Liselotte*, p. 48, 26 January 1688.

44. Franklin, *La Vie privée*, XVIII, *Les Magasins*, III, p. 226.

45. Don Fader, 'The "Cabale du Dauphin", Campra, and Italian comedy: the courtly politics of French musical patronage around 1700', pp. 400–401.

L'Angelique

Another lute/guitar-register piece. An *angélique* is a type of lute not unlike the theorbo, and it is perhaps significant that, for his only piece in the *Pièces de Clavecin* named after a musical instrument, Couperin should have chosen a relatively obscure term, and one that is so open to double meaning in a way that *luth* or *théorbe* would not be. Perhaps a secondary meaning refers to Angelo Costantini, Mezzetin of the Comédiens Italiens, always portrayed playing his guitar, and brother-in-law of Spinette (*L'Epineuse*) of the *Twenty-sixth Ordre*. Another candidate is a singer:

> Philémon, son of a rich German merchant, attached himself to Angélique, a singer at the Opéra. He attended all the rehearsals, courting his mistress at the theatre. He adored her, spending a lot on her, imagining himself having an affair with a Lucretia, whereas this beauty was the most debauched of all the girls of this sort.[46]

Yet another possibility is Angélique Houssu, a brilliant harpsichordist, and wife of Antoine Forqueray.

La Villers

Christophe-Alexandre Pajot de Villers, dedicatee and financer of the engraving of *Book I.* He was Contrôleur Général des Postes et Relais de France and lived near Couperin at Saint-Germain. In 1713 he married Anne de Mailly. Perhaps this accounts for the two parts of the piece – an engagement present perhaps.

Les Vendangeuses

The wine harvesters. Another tipsy dance like *Enjoüemens Bachiques* (*Fourth Ordre*). A common scene in *divertissements* and plays.

46. Nemeitz, *Séjour*, p. 45. The specific identity of these two is not known.

Les Agrémens

One of the longest of all the pieces, a distinction it shares with *Les Brinborions* (*Twenty-fourth Ordre*). Both *agréments* and *brimborions* (the correct spellings), according to Furetière, were feminine ornaments: 'Quelques ornemens qu'on met sur l'habit, sur un visage, mouches, cheveux bouclez qui accompagnent les temples' ('Ornaments that they put on a coat, on a face, face-spots, curls which adorn the temples'). One of Couperin's humorous comments on female vanity, it is evidently a common eighteenth-century joke, since Handel uses it in *Semele*, where the heroine admires herself in the mirror in the inordinately long aria, 'Myself I shall adore'.

Les Ondes

Nymphs of the waves, who often appeared in *divertissements*. Possibly a reference to boats making for Cythera, a popular subject for ballets at the time.[47]

BOOK II (1717)

Sixième Ordre

Les Moissonneurs

This *ordre*, like those in *Book I*, has the air of a *divertissement*. It may be coincidence, but several of the pieces could well apply to the Duchesse Du Maine. In 1714 a pastoral *divertissement*, *Le Mystère ou les Fêtes de l'Inconnu*, was put on at Sceaux. Among *Le Mystère*'s followers were *moissonneurs* (harvesters). *Les Moissonneurs*

---

47. See Georgia Cowart, 'Watteau's *Pilgrimage to Cythera* and the subversive utopia of the opera-ballet'.

is a piece of contrasts, the peasant dance with the sophisticated *couplet*.

Les Langueurs-Tendres

The love-lorn sighs. Madame Du Maine prided herself on Sceaux being an up-dated version of the seventeenth-century salons, which set out to refine manners but which in the end became so ridiculously precious that Molière had to send the whole preposterous apparatus up in *Les Précieuses ridicules*. They preached, as someone put it, a refinement of love and a love of refinement, a subtlety of sighing for the unattainable lover. Madeleine de Scudéry went as far as to analyse the twelve types of sigh and the nine grades of esteem. She drew a map of love, *La Carte de Tendre*, to guide the sighing swains and their drooping admirers. From *Nouvelle Amitié* three routes led to *Tendre-sur-Estime*, *Tendre-sur-Reconnaissance* and *Tendre-sur-Inclination*. Villages on the route had delicious names like *Grand Esprit* or *Billet Doux*. If *Les Langueurs-Tendres* does not refer to the Duchesse Du Maine, who was held to have a tender affection for the poet Malézieu, Couperin is poking gentle fun at someone in a similar situation, but so subtly that were they to play the piece they would be unaware of the composer's amusement.

Le Gazoüillement

The chattering of birds. Possibly another portrait of Madame Du Maine and her friends, who were known as *Les Oiseaux de Sceaux*.[48] The conversation of the Duchess was said to be a bright, shallow, witty stream of monologue. In fact she said of herself that she loved society, everyone listened to her and she listened to no one.[49]

48. André Maurel, *La Duchesse du Maine Reine de Sceaux*, p. 58.
49. Marguerite Glotz and Madeleine Maire, *Salons du XVIIIe siècle*, p. 65.

La Bersan

André Bauyn, Seigneur de Bersan, a tax farmer and owner of the famous Bauyn manuscript, one of the most important sources of keyboard music by Couperin's uncle, Louis Couperin. A down-to-earth contrast to the preciosity of the previous piece. The music suggests that Seigneur de Bersan is laughing.

Les Baricades Mistérieuses

This could be another reference to *Le Mystère ou les Fêtes de l'Inconnu* (see *Les Moissonneurs* above). The Duchesse Du Maine, the inspiration behind the show and the mysterious presence, addressed the company masked, and it is more than possible that *Les Baricades Mistérieuses* are indeed masks. Possibly a reference to Freemasonry; the incessant groups of three notes reinforce this possibility (see *La Visionaire* and *La Misterieuse, Twenty-fifth Ordre*).

Les Bergeries

The shepherds of the pastoral *divertissement*. Again there is a contrast between the naïve *rondeau* and the sophisticated *couplets*. When she was over fifty the Duchesse Du Maine was still playing the *ingénue* shepherdess in a love-affair with the gentle shepherd Houdar de la Motte.

La Commére

A common woman. Furetière: 'Femme de basse condition qui s'ingère de parler de tout et qui veut savoir toutes les nouvelles de quartier' ('Common woman who wants to know all the news of the neighbourhood in order to gossip about it'). Again a contrast.

Le Moucheron

Possibly yet another in-joke referring to the Duchesse Du Maine. In *La Tarentole* at Châtenay, in which Marguerite-Louise Couperin sang and Couperin may have played, she played the servant Finemouche, which means a sly minx (see p. 23). A *moucheron* is a very small fly, another allusion to her minuteness. The nickname refers to the emblem of the honey bee (see *L'Abeille, First Ordre*), as a verse from the show reveals:

> L'abeille, petit animal,
> > Fait de grandes blessures,
> Craignez son aiguillon fatal,
> > Évitez ses piqûres;
> Fuyez, si vous pouvez, les traits
> > Qui partent de sa bouche,
> Elle pique et s'envole après:
> > C'est une Finemouche.[50]

(The bee, a little animal, makes great wounds, fear its fatal sting, avoid its pricks; fly, if you can, from the arrows that shoot from its mouth, it stings and flies away afterwards: it is a sly minx.)

A sly and sophisticated piece compared to *La Commére*.

Septième Ordre

La Ménetou

Françoise Charlotte de Ménethoud, a prodigy who sang, danced, played the flute and the harpsichord and appeared before the King in 1689, aged nine. She was also a composer: in 1691 fifteen *Airs sérieux à deux* were published by the royal printer Christophe Ballard, making her, at the age of only eleven, the youngest female composer ever to have her works published in France.[51] She appears in many satirical poems:

> Ce n'est point la taille charmante
> De la Menetou qui m'enchante,

---

50. Cessac, 'Un portrait musical de la duchesse du Maine (1676–1753)', p. 43.
51. David Chung, 'Patronage and the development of French harpsichord music during Louis XIV's reign', p. 114.

> Ni son clavecin, ni son chant,
> Ni sa mine grimacière.
> Mais c'est qu'elle est à quatorze ans,
>   Plus putain que fut sa mère.[52]

(It is not the charming figure of La Ménethoud that enchants me, nor her harpsichord, nor her singing, nor her grimacing face. But it is that at fourteen she is more of a whore than her mother was.)

And in a Noel of 1696, when twenty ladies of the court filed to the chapel at Versailles 'en dévotes' to pay their respects to the Christ child, each carrying a little lantern:

> La Menetou s'avance
> Disant à sa Maman
> Faudra-t-il que je danse
> Devant le Saint enfant?
> La duchesse répond,
> Mettons tout en besogne,
> Flutons, dansons, chantons, sautons,
> Joseph nous mariera, la la,
>   Aux princes de Pologne.[53]

(La Ménethoud advances, saying to her mother, do I have to dance before the Holy Child? The duchess replies, let us set to work, let us play the flute, dance, sing, jump, Joseph will marry us to the princes of Poland.)

La Ménethoud's mother was the Duchesse de La Ferté, one of the habituées at Sceaux. She married the Duc de La Ferté in 1675 and he did not die until 1703, so this must be an in-joke. She was an impulsive and somewhat eccentric and unpredictable lady whose intense attachments to people tended to be of a temporary nature. She was separated from her husband, against whom she wrote a wicked verse which was popular in Paris. Mademoiselle Pélissier,

52. Maurepas, *Recueil*, II, p. 174.
53. Maurepas, *Recueil*, II, p. 273.

the celebrated singer who sang for Rameau, was an illegitimate daughter of La Ménethoud and was in her turn the lover of the violinist Francœur.[54]

Les Petits Ages:
  La Muse Naissante
  L'Enfantine
  L'Adolescente
  Les Délices

Possibly again referring to Madame de Ménethoud. Furetière: 'Les Délices du cœur sont plus touchantes que celles de l'esprit' ('The delights of the heart are more touching that those of the spirit').

La Basque

A dancer at the Opéra was known as La Basque.[55] In 1700 a *fête à la Basque* was given for the Dauphin at the Hôtel de Gramont, the Duc de Gramont dancing *à la Basque*.[56]

La Chazé

Presumably a member of the family from the chateau of Chazé sur Argos in Maine et Loire.

Les Amusemens

Couperin's preoccupation with the two sides of life is constantly in evidence. This magnificent piece in two parts may well be a reference to *Les Amusemens sérieux et comiques* by Dufresny (see *Les Vieux Seigneurs* and *Les Jeunes Seigneurs, Twenty-fourth Ordre*). Furetière: 'Galanteries, badinage. Il est bon d'egayer la tristesse des leçons et de les deguiser en badinage' ('Gallantries towards the ladies, playfulness. It is good to lighten the sadness of lessons and

54. Maurepas, *Recueil*, IV, pp. 4–5.
55. Maurepas, *Recueil*, I, p. 251.
56. Fader, 'The "Cabale du Dauphin"', p. 390.

to disguise them in playfulness'). This is true of the first half of *Les Amusemens*, but nothing can disguise the sadness of the second, which is worthy of Schubert.

Huitiême Ordre

The architecture of this *ordre* is discussed on p. 98.

La Raphaéle

Since this *ordre* is in Couperin's *goûts-réunis* style, a style in which he sought to join the French and Italian styles in music, the title may refer to the artist Raphael, whose paintings were the great pride of Parisian collectors. Watteau's patron, the banker Pierre Crozat, brought Raphaels back from Urbino and took a delight in showing them. He held frequent musical evenings at his *hôtel* at which Couperin must have played. Couperin could also have seen a Raphael in one of the Jacobite collections at Saint-Germain. Painting was one of the topics discussed at the salons (see p. 37). The Regent also had a very important picture collection which included Raphaels. Couperin must have known this collection well too. Chromaticism, considered by the French to be an entirely Italian characteristic, is prevalent in the *ordre*. In this allemande Couperin also makes use of short, declamatory figures borrowed from Italian vocal music.

Allemande L'Ausoniéne

Ausonia was an ancient poetic name for Italy. This is an Italian-type *allemande légère*. It could also be a reference to the Duc de Bourgogne, Couperin's pupil, one of whose titles was Seigneur d'Ausone, often written Ausonne.[57]

57. Pierre Citron, *Couperin*, p. 95.

Premiere Courante
Seconde Courante

In both these contrasted courantes (see *First Ordre*, p. 104) the smooth lines of the French courante are interrupted by angular, declamatory Italian figures.

Sarabande L'Unique

This grave dance is punctuated by sudden changes of tempo, present in the Italian string sonatas which Couperin would have heard at the Stuart court at Saint-Germain-en-Laye. This Sarabande also fits a description of a male solo sarabande from 1671: 'First he danced with charming grace, serious and cautious, in a regular and slow rhythm, with noble, beautiful, free and easy bearing [...] from time to time he allowed a rhythmic unit to pass, thereby remaining as still as a statue, and then, flying away like an arrow, he appeared suddenly at the other end of the room'.[58]

Gavotte

See *First Ordre*, p. 105.

Rondeau

A truly French piece.

Gigue

In his chamber music Couperin marks this type of gigue to be played *d'une légéreté modérée*.

Passacaille

After a typically French gigue this passacaille is a great fusion of French and Italian styles (see p. 98).

---

58. Père François Pomey, in *Dictionnaire royal augmenté* (1671). I am grateful to Ludmila Tschakalova for this reference.

La Morinéte

Jean Baptiste Morin, who, to quote Corrette, 'following the lead of the Italians, wrote the first French cantatas.'[59] He combined French melodies with Italian harmonies, so creating his own *goûts-réunis* style. He was famous for his detachable 'alleluya' finales, one in the form of a vocal gigue.

In contrast to the *Seventh Ordre*, this one is full of drama. Whilst the gentle and peaceful *Seventh Ordre* ends in tragedy, Couperin 'lightens' the 'lessons' of the *Eighth* with one of the most gently beguiling pieces of all.

Neuvième Ordre

Allemande à deux Clavecins

To judge by the rest of the *ordre* this allemande has amorous connotations.

La Rafraîchissante

The cooling off.

Les Charmes

A piece in the lute style. The lute was considered an aid in love and lutenists were supposed to have special charm. Furetière: 'Elle a des charmes et des attraits qui asservissent tous les cœurs' ('She has charms and attractions that enslave every heart').

La Princesse de Sens

Probably Élisabeth-Thérèse-Alexandrine de Bourbon, the Duchesse Du Maine's niece, known as Mademoiselle de Sens. Couperin

---

59. David Tunley, *The Eighteenth-Century French Cantata*, p. 14.

taught her two elder sisters, so presumably he taught her as well. She never married.

L'Olimpique

Possibly, as has always been suggested, Olympe de Brouilly, wife of the Duc d'Aumont, principal churchwarden at Saint Gervais. She was said to be vain and haughty.[60] Both she and her husband were famous for their love affairs; the Duke was said to have had affairs with both Thérèse and Mimi Dancourt. Or perhaps the subject is the Duchesse Du Maine; at Sceaux, tributes to her were sung in which she was referred to as a compound of all the goddesses of Olympus.

L'Insinüante

Perhaps some shy member of the Bourbon-Condé family who could only suggest her sentiments with hesitations.

> ISABELLE: Pour mes maniéres elles sont douces & insinuantes.[61]

> (ISABELLE: As for my manners, they are gentle and modest.)

Furetière: 'Qui entre doucement dans l'esprit de quelqu'un, qui est doux, honnête, engageant' ('Someone who enters gently into a person's spirit, who is meek, honest, pleasing').

La Séduisante

A seductive lady, perhaps again a member of this family.

Le Bavolet-flotant

A seductive ribbon that floated on ladies' backs. Furetière: 'Vous voulez faire voir dans vos trophées amoureux des bavolets' ('You want to show some *bavolets* among your amorous trophies').

---

60. Maurepas, *Recueil*, II, p. 296.
61. Regnard, *La Coquette*, in Gherardi, *Théâtre italien*, III, p. 130.

Le Petit-deüil, ou les Trois Veuves

Half-mourning. *Deüil de Cour: le grand deüil* lasted from two to six months; *le petit deüil* from three days to three months, depending on the wish of the King. The word *veuve* ('widow') was used figuratively to mean someone who is deprived of lovers. Probably the three unmarried daughters of Monsieur le Duc, Louise-Anne de Bourbon (Mademoiselle de Charolais), Marie-Anne de Bourbon (Mademoiselle de Clermont) and Mademoiselle de Sens. These three sisters were evidently something of a joke, since they appear in a poem in which La Charolaise was intended for the King and Mesdemoiselles de Clermont and de Sens were searching for husbands in Spain.[62]

Menuet

This is an Italian minuet. Brossard, in his *Dictionnaire de musique* of 1703, says: 'On devroit à l'imitation des Italiens se servir du signe 3/8 ou 6/8 pour en marquer le mouvement, qui est toujours gay et fort vite' ('One should, in imitation of the Italians, use the sign 3/8 or 6/8 to mark the time, which is always gay and very quick').

Dixième Ordre

La Triomphante:
    Bruit de Guerre
    Alégrésse des Vainqueurs
    Fanfare

In three sections, the first being sub-titled *Bruit de Guerre* ('noise of war'). In 1712 Ballard published a book of drinking songs which

62. Maurepas, *Recueil*, III, p. 350.

he called *Tendresses bachiques*. Despite the gentle title the collection is full of mock-battles. The words of one of them begin:

> Quel désordre, quel bruit de guerre,
> Attaquons ces fiers ennemis,
> Que leur sang coule dans le verre.

(What disorder, what rumours of war, let's attack our bold enemies so that their blood flows in the glass.)

The arpeggiated figures in bars 36–9 and 44–7 imitate trumpet calls (see also *Les Calotines, Nineteenth Ordre*, bars 29–32).

The next section of *La Triomphante* is *Alégrésse des Vainqueurs*, a typical *tendresse bachique*, ending with 'blood flowing in the glass'.[63] The final section of this *bacchanale* is a *Fanfare*. These appear in the Ballard collection too, and the words urge everyone to drink to the victory.

La Mézangére

Antoine Scott, Seigneur de Mézangère, one of the King's *maîtres d'hôtel*. Given the context, this may portray him lurching about after too much wine. His wife, Élisabeth, was a pupil of Couperin and involved in Crozat's concerts.[64] They both figure in satirical poems like the following:

> Pour ta volière,
> Adorable Moineau,
> La Mézangère
> Est un plaisant oiseau.[65]

(For your aviary, adorable sparrow, the tit is a pleasant bird.)

---

63. Ludmila Tschakalova suggests flowing wine rather than bells of victory for the semiquavers.

64. Lowell Lindgren, 'Parisian patronage of performers from the Royal Academy of Musick (1719–28)', p. 17.

65. Maurepas, *Recueil*, V, p. 243.

Couperin's piece is not at all typical of those he dedicates to amorous ladies, so its subject is likely to be the husband, whose appearances in these verses are untranslatable.[66]

La Gabriéle

Gabriel-Vincent Thévenard was a celebrated singer, who worked with Couperin (see p. 40). 'Never had a musician better understood the art of singing.' His drinking habits were also famous: 'He swallowed quantities of wine on the specious pretext that it strengthened his voice.'[67] The grandest ladies threw themselves at him, and the greatest nobles 'invited him to their tables where he drank as well as he sang'.[68] A proud man, when told by the English ambassador that his sovereign would like to see and hear him, he replied: 'Monsieur, I represent him and his kind at the Opéra three times a week.' Legends about him abound but Lecerf de La Viéville gives a very interesting description of his singing; he was clearly a very distinguished artist.[69] He is the subject of many satirical verses, sometimes under his nickname, Le Comte d'Holstein Ploen:

> Du comte d'Holstein Ploen
> Faut tous chanter la gloire;
> On le voit souvent boire
> Avec Lorge et Bouillon
> Le Comte d'Holstein Ploen.[70]

(Everyone has to sing to the glory of the Comte d'Holstein Ploen; one often sees him drinking with the Duc de Lorge and the Chevalier de Bouillon.)

66. Maurepas, *Recueil*, III, p. 119.

67. Campardon, *L'Académie Royale au XVIIIᵉ siècle*, II, p. 307.

68. Le Brisoys Desnoiresterres, *Cours Galantes*, III, p. 213.

69. Campardon, *L'Académie Royale*, II, pp. 307–8.

70. Maurepas, *Recueil*, III, p. 72.

A catalogue of his impressive music library survives and reveals that he possessed both Couperin's *Pièces de Clavecin* and his *Concerts Royaux.*[71]

La Nointéle

Perhaps Jean de Turmenies, Seigneur de Nointel, Garde du Trésor Royal, but far more likely Louis de Béchameil, Marquis de Nointel, another of Louis XIV's *maîtres d'hôtel* and a wealthy financier. The dining room of his Paris *hôtel* was decorated by Watteau. The figures represented drinking and the comedy; they included Bacchus, a drinker, a wine harvester, Folly and Momus (god of satire).[72] Béchamel sauce is named after him, though he did not invent it; he merely perfected an old recipe. Since Couperin possessed four volumes of a *Cuisinier françois* ('*The French Cook*') he may have appreciated Béchameil's interests.[73]

La Fringante

Furetière: 'Cheval bien fringant, difficile à monter et à manier' ('A frisky horse, difficult to mount and to handle'). Marked to be played *relevé*, which, when applied to horses, is defined by Furetière as 'Les mouvements d'un cheval qui s'élève plus haut que la terre à terre' ('The movements of a horse that picks its feet up higher than the commonplace'). This and the following piece must apply to Mademoiselle Maupin, who was an excellent horsewoman in addition to the attributes mentioned below (for the implications of horse-riding see *La Babet, Second Ordre*, and the canon *La Femme entre deux Draps* on p. 33).

71. Albert Cohen, '"Un cabinet de musique" – the library of an eighteenth-century musician'.

72. Jean Cailleaux, 'Decorations by Watteau for the hôtel de Nointel', *Burlington Magazine* 103 (March 1961), No. 696, Supplement, pp. i–v.

73. Michel Antoine, 'Autour de François Couperin', p. 123.

L'Amazône

Mademoiselle Maupin, another distinguished singer who worked with Couperin (see p. 28). 'One of the most valiant Amazons you could find.' She loved to dress up as a man, had affairs with men and women alike and 'had a natural taste for the use of arms', fighting duels in which she defeated at least three men; she fell in love with Fanchon Moreau (see *La Tendre Fanchon, Fifth Ordre*) and tried to commit suicide when she was rejected. She was, however, not large, very pretty and married.[74] Legends about her abound and she inspired Théophile Gautier's novel *Mademoiselle de Maupin*. No one seems sure of her Christian name, but her maiden name was d'Aubigny, Maupin being the surname of her husband. She made her professional singing début in Marseilles under her maiden name. On her way back to Paris she met Gabriel-Vincent Thévenard, who was also hoping to pursue a career as a singer; they both became stars. La Maupin was a contralto and when Campra wrote the part of Clorinde in his opera *Tancrède* for her in 1702 it was the first opera in Paris with a female lead who was not a soprano.

Les Bagatelles

Trifles, perhaps indicating the frivolous tone of the *ordre*; but such a beautiful piece surely recognizes the significance of trifles.

> Il ne faut qu'une bagatelle
> Pour estre heureux ou malheureux;
> Pour faire un infidelle
> De l'Amant le plus amoureux,
> Il ne faut qu'une bagatelle.[75]

(It only needs a bagatelle to make you happy or miserable, or to make the most amorous lover unfaithful.)

74. Campardon, *L'Académie Royale*, II, p. 178.
75. Boisfran, *Arlequin misanthrope*, in Gherardi, *Théâtre italien*, VI, p. 521.

Onzième Ordre

La Castelane

The Marquis de Castellane was the Duc Du Maine's Chamberlain. His wife was involved in Crozat's concerts.[76]

L'Etincelante ou La Bontems
Les Graces-Naturéles, Suite de La Bontems

As Couperin said in his prefaces, many of the pieces in *Books I* and *II* had been written for twenty years before they were published. This must be true of this piece and of the *Fastes de la Grande et Ancienne Ménéstrandise* (see below). The Bontemps family were the King's *valets de chambre* for several generations. The one portrayed here is Alexandre Bontemps, who had the adventure described by Couperin in 1691, just before the affair of the *Ménéstrandise*. The gold fringes from the curtains of the antechamber to the State Apartments at Versailles were stolen. Bontemps was, naturally, furious and desperate to get them back. Next day at supper, 'something big and black', as Saint Simon describes it, 'fell on the table in front of the King and Madame. The impact was so violent that all the dishes vibrated, but none was overturned. There was a moment of panic: one might have feared an attempt upon the King's life. The King alone was perfectly admirable in his coolness and serenity. He half-turned his head and remarked "I think these are my fringes". Pinned to the parcel was a note: "Take back your fringes Bontemps. They are more of a bore than a pleasure. I kiss the King's hand"'.[77] So close to the King, Bontemps was in an influential position, but unlike many

76. Lowell Lindgren, 'Parisian patronage of performers from the Royal Academy of Musick', p. 17.

77. Jacques Levron, *Daily Life at Versailles*, p. 92.

courtiers, he never abused his position. Saint Simon is unusually unstinted in his praise: 'He harmed no-one and always used his influence for good. Great numbers of people owed their fortunes to him and he was modest almost to the point of breaking with them if they so much as mentioned it. He loved procuring favours solely for the pleasure of it.'[78] *Les Graces-Naturéles* is a phrase that might most readily be taken to refer to feminine beauty or 'natural charms', but the sub-title shows us that here it clearly means *grâces* in the sense of favours or thanks. Furetière: 'Faveur qu'un supérieur fait à un inférieur' ('A favour granted by a superior to an inferior'). Furetière also explains that *naturel* can mean *véritable* ('genuine'). *Affectueusement* must be used in its genuine, affectionate, meaning here, for the music shows no hint of irony or double meaning. An important man, Bontemps was Governor of the town of Versailles and had many other responsibilities, including the administration of buildings and hunts.

La Zénobie

Crébillon's play *Rhadamist(h)e et Zénobie* was first performed in 1711, and seems at the time to have been regarded as his master-piece. The plot of the tragedy is notoriously impenetrable, but the main point is that Zénobie is in love with her brother-in-law. Couperin probably had a particular candidate in mind. Alter-natively it is likely that he is referring to Zenobia as Queen of Palmyra, as portrayed by La Bruyère, heroically facing a hostile enemy after the death of her husband. He could have related this to the Marquise de Lambert, who, after the death of her husband (with whom she had been very happy) in 1686, faced lengthy and troublesome lawsuits against his family to save her children's property. Historically Zenobia, defeated by the Romans, was taken hostage to Rome. The emperor Aurelian was so impressed by her

78. *Saint Simon*, I, p. 146.

that he set her free, granting her a villa at Tivoli where she held literary salons, surrounding herself with philosophers and poets. The Marquise de Lambert, with her own famous salon, was thus following in her footsteps. The oratory of Cicero, 'O tempora, O mores', was often parodied, and the rhetorical figures that begin halfway through bar 24 may be a musical imitation.

Les Fastes de la grande et ancienne Mxnxstrxndxsx:
  Premier Acte; Les Notables et Jurés Mxnxstrxndxurs
  Second Acte; Les Viéleux et les Gueux
  Troisiême Acte; Les Jongleurs, Sauteurs et Saltimbanques, avec les Ours et les Singes
  Quatriême Acte; Les Invalides, ou gens Estropiés au Service de la grande Mxnxstrxndxsx
  Cinquiême Acte; Désordre et déroute de toute la troupe, causés par les Yvrognes, les Singes et les Ours.

Couperin's other battle, *Les Fastes de la grande et ancienne Ménéstrandise*, is a very different affair from *Bruit de Guerre* of the previous *ordre*. Gone is the light-hearted world of Bacchus; we are in the bitter and perennial world of the closed shop. The *Ménéstrandise* dated from 1321 and its other title was the Community of Dancing Masters and Instrumentalists of the String Consort & the Oboe, in other words, an ancient guild. Its members included jugglers, conjurors, hurdy-gurdy players and minstrels, which included poets, as well as the Vingt-Quatre Violons du Roi. One of the privileges of the guild was that any member could cross the Petit Pont into Paris without paying a toll, in exchange for singing a song or having his monkey perform a trick. Gradually various branches broke away, finding the original rules of the guild too restrictive. In 1693 the *Ménéstrandise* decided that all harpsichordists must join. They refused and were imprisoned in the Châtelet, whereupon they appealed to the courts of justice. The four organists of the Royal Chapel, Lebègue, Nivers,

Buterne and Couperin, intervened on behalf of the composers, organists and harpsichordists and won the case; the *Ménéstrandise* had to pay costs.

Couperin's music is a bitter satire on the pomposity of the elders (Act I) and on the standard of the members, whom he portrays as beggars with their hurdy-gurdies (Act II), jugglers, tumblers and buffoons with their monkeys and their bears (Act III), and invalids and cripples (Act IV). These are vicious caricatures. In the end they are all sent flying in a triumphant finale, scattered by the monkeys and the bears who are aided by the drunks (Act V).

Douzième Ordre

Les Juméles

The twins. Probably the inseparable Loyson sisters (see p. 50, *Les Nonètes*, *First Ordre*, and *Les Chérubins ou L'aimable Lazure*, *Twentieth Ordre*). Many potential victims were saved by the fact that they were always together; La Sablière wrote:

> Ces deux sœurs d'égalle beauté
> De tous les cœurs ont fait partage.
> Je garde seul ma liberté
> Parmi ce public esclavage.
> Tout ce qu'on voit de précieux
> En leurs personnes se rassemble.
> Ce qui m'a sauvé de leurs yeux,
> C'est qu'elles sont toujours ensemble.

(These two sisters of equal beauty have divided all hearts between them. I alone remain free amid this general enslavement. They have all their precious attributes in common. What has saved me from the spell cast by their eyes is that they are always together.)

Fontenelle shared the indecision of many:

> Quatre beaux yeux m'ont su charmer;
> Ah! Mon mal ne vient que d'aimer.
> Deux sœurs que je n'ose nommer
> Me tournent la cervelle.
> Ah! Mon mal ne vient que d'aimer
> Mais je ne sais laquelle. [79]

(Four beautiful eyes have been able to charm me; ah! my pain is due only to love. Two sisters whom I dare not name have turned my head. Ah! my pain is due only to love, but I don't know which one.)

L'Intîme, Mouvement de Courante

See *First Ordre*, p. 104, for the amorous connotations in courantes.

La Galante

A *mouche* (patch) worn in the middle of the cheek.[80] The use of *mouches* was often mocked in comedies, as in the following scene:

> OCTAVE (tirant une boëtte à mouches de sa poche), to Mezzetin, his valet: Je crois qu'une petite mouche ne me sieroit pas mal là. Tiens, place-la toy-mesme, frote bien ta main, & ne me salis point le visage.
> MEZZETIN en haussant les épaules: Quel homme! Donnez. La voila bien.
> OCTAVE se regardant dans le miroir: Coquin, tu me l'as mise sur le bout du nez!
> MEZZETIN: Elle est bien là, Monsieur, pour estre veue de plus loin.[81]

(OCTAVE (taking a box of patches from his pocket): I think a little *mouche* would be good there. Here, you put it there, wipe your hands well and don't dirty my face.)

79. Alexandre Calame, *Regnard, sa vie et son œuvre*, p. 87.
80. Franklin, *La Vie privée*, II, *Les Soins de la Toilette*, p. 96.
81. Palaprat, *La Fille de bon sens*, in Gherardi, *Théâtre italien*, IV, p. 128.

MEZZETIN shrugging his shoulders: What a man! Give it me. There
you are.
OCTAVE looking at himself in the mirror: Ass, you have put it on the
end of my nose!
MEZZETIN: It's good there, Sir, it can be seen from a long way off.)

La Coribante

Corybantes were an orgiastic sect of Greek priests. In this piece
Philippe d'Orléans, Regent of France, makes his first appearance.
His nocturnal habits were very different from the Duchesse Du
Maine's: there was no question of sighing for unattainable lovers.
However, as at Sceaux, the guests at his *soupers des déesses* did
assume mythological characters, and the actions did take place in a
symbolical world. Fauns and satyrs laid the tables, Juno and
Minerva helped in the kitchen. Rank disappeared; everyone did his
bit. Dukes and duchesses rubbed shoulders (and a great deal more
besides) with chorus girls and carpenters. The party started, at any
rate after he had assumed the leadership of France, on the dot of
nine o'clock. Catastrophic despatches might arrive and provinces
might revolt but no one could get at the Regent until his official
levée the following morning. Amazingly, this brilliant man still
managed to govern the country. If Couperin, as a musician, was
involved in these orgies we do not know. Probably he was like
Ibagnat, the porter at the Palais Royal, whose duty it was to light
the Regent to the door of the supper room. On one occasion his
master laughingly invited the porter to join him, to which Ibagnat
austerely replied: 'Monseigneur, my duty ends at this door; I must
respectfully decline to wait on such bad company and I am very
sorry to see Your Highness in it.'[82]

82. W. H. Lewis, *Sunset*, p. 258.

La Vauvré

Madame de Vauvré, who showed the young Mademoiselle de Launay great kindness when she first arrived in Paris. Mademoiselle de Launay found, on her first visit: 'A woman of extraordinary appearance but one possessed of much intelligence.' Madame de Vauvré was civilized, kind and considerate. She lived beside the Jardin des Simples, then a physic garden and now the Botanical Gardens. Because of the remote situation she saw few visitors, but she had distinguished friends, including the anatomist Joseph-Guichard Duverney, who was a neighbour. She and Mademoiselle de Launay became great friends, and one of their delights was walking either in her garden or in the Simples, of which she had a key.[83] A charming and innocent piece, in contrast to *La Coribante*.

La Fileuse

The spinner. Spinning had amorous connotations. The tongue-in-cheek *naïveté* is a contrast to the genuine charm of *La Vauvré*. The subject also of a painting by Watteau (see p. 41).

La Boulonoise

Perhaps a reference to a member of the Duc d'Aumont's family. As well as being principal churchwarden of Saint Gervais the Duke was governor of Boulogne.

L'Atalante

In Greek mythology Atalanta was not interested in marriage and only agreed to it on condition her suitors could outrun her in a race. Melanion asked the goddess Aphrodite for help and she gave him golden apples to drop as Atalanta caught up. In this piece

---

83. Madame de Staal de Launay, *Memoirs*, I, pp. 88–90.

Couperin cleverly describes the race; the running semiquavers suddenly come to a halt at a cadence as Atalanta picks up the apples. Possibly a reference to someone who was always in a hurry and always dropping things.

BOOK III (1722)

Treiziéme Ordre

Les Lis naissans

The birth of the lilies, the *Fleur de lis* being the emblem of the Kingdom of France, also the emblem of purity. Furetière: 'Se dit figurément et poetiquement du Royaume de France' ('Said figuratively and poetically of the Kingdom of France'). The whole of this *ordre* refers to Philippe, Duc d'Orléans (see also *La Coribante*, *Twelfth Ordre*, and *La Régente ou La Minerve*, *Fifteenth Ordre*) who became Regent of France on the death of his uncle, Louis XIV. This complex man has come down in history as a thoroughly bad lot, but this is not by any means the whole truth. In the same unfortunate position as the Prince de Conti (see the *Sixteenth Ordre*), he had his wings clipped. The highly critical Saint Simon writes of the Duke in sadly sympathetic terms:

> When his ambitions were thwarted he took pride in licentiousness. The rakes of Paris gained a hold over him. Resentment at being forced into an unsuitable marriage drove him to seek consolation elsewhere. Disappointment at being refused the command of an army and the governorships and other offices he had been promised finally led him into dissolute living which he carried to extremes in order to show a contempt for his wife and the King's displeasure.[84]

84. *Saint Simon*, I, p. 195.

His wife was one of the King's illegitimate daughters, a match that the Orléans family considered a slight.

Les Rozeaux

The reeds, emblems of human frailty. As Pascal said: 'Man is only a reed, the weakest thing in nature.'[85] Furetière: 'Un esprit faible qui plit comme un roseau' ('A weak spirit that bends like a reed').

L'engageante

Furetière: 'Un nœud de ruban de couleur jaune que les jeunes demoiselles portent sur le sein' ('A bow of yellow ribbon that young ladies wear on their breast'). Also: 'Ces manches galantes laissant voir de beaux bras ont le nom d'engageantes'[86] ('Elegant sleeves which allow beautiful arms to be seen have the name *engageantes*'). Furetière warns: 'Il faut donner de garde des caresses des femmes, elles sont trop engageantes' ('It is necessary to beware of the caresses of women, they are too tempting'). The frail reed gives way.

Les Folies françoises ou Les Dominos:

La Virginité sous le Domino couleur d'invisible
La Pudeur sous le Domino couleur de Roze
L'Ardeur sous le Domino incarnat
L'Espérance sous le Domino Vert
La Fidelité sous le Domino Bleu
La Persévérance sous le Domino Gris de lin
La Langueur sous le Domino Violet
La Coquéterie sous diférens Dominos

85. David Maland, *Culture and Society in Seventeenth-Century France*, p. 190.
86. Franklin, *La Vie privée*, XV, *Les Magasins*, I, p. 239.

Les Vieux galans et les Trésorieres Suranées sous les Dominos
  Pourpres, et feuilles mortes
Les Coucous Bénévoles sous les Dominos jaunes
Le Jalousie Taciturne sous le Domino gris de maure
La Frénésie, ou le Désespoir sous le Domino noir
L'âme-en peine

Les Folies françoises is a set of tiny variations loosely based on the famous *Folies d'Espagne*. Each variation is a character at a masked ball and each wears a different-coloured domino (cloak). The Regent held masked balls at the Opéra three times a week, but eventually they caused such a scandal they had to be banned. First of all, Virginity appears in an invisible domino. 'Invisible' implied someone who was undressing and was unwilling to be seen. Next come Modesty, blushing in a pink domino, Ardour in a flesh-coloured domino and Hope in a green one. Fidelity wears a blue domino and Perseverance a flaxen grey (silver) one. Languor in a purple domino is followed by Coquetry in different dominos. The old gallants and the pensioned-off courtesans limp around wearing crimson dominos and verdigris *(feuilles mortes, vert de gris)*[87] but unlike the vicious caricature of the old crocks in the *Ménéstrandise* (see the *Eleventh Ordre*), Couperin's portrait of these ancient *roués* is one of humorous compassion. Next we have the benevolent cuckolds in yellow dominos, and, by contrast, taciturn jealousy in a Moorish (dark) grey one, doubtless a reference to the legendary jealousy of Moorish captors of European maidens. Everything ends in frenzy and despair, in black. All these characters work their way to their inevitable doom, *L'âme-en peine* ('the soul in torment'). Though this tragic *ordre* must refer to the Regent, it could also have been intended as a warning to the young Louis XV.

87. Franklin, *La Vie privée*, XVIII, *Les Magasins*, III, p. 75.

Quatorziéme Ordre

Le Rossignol-en-amour, Double du Rossignol
All the bird pieces in this *ordre* refer to various amorous states.
They may hark back to the Duchesse Du Maine and *Les Oiseaux
de Sceaux* (see *Sixth Ordre*). The nightingale was always associated
with love. See p. 47.

La Linote-éfarouchée
The startled linnet.

Les Fauvétes Plaintives
The plaintive warblers.

Le Rossignol-Vainqueur
The victorious nightingale.

La Julliet
July is often spelt in this way. Furetière: proverbially 'en Juillet la
faucille au poignet' ('The sickle at the wrist'). Possibly a reference
to the conquering nightingale's harvest.

Le Carillon de Cithére
Cythera was the island of love (see *Les Pélerines, Third Ordre*).

Le Petit-Rien
Perhaps implies, like *Les Bagatelles* (*Tenth Ordre*), that this *ordre*
consists of trifles.

Peint par Santerre.

B.R

Gravé par F.ⁿ Guibert

LE RÉGENT.

Philippe d'Orléans as Regent of France, with Marie-Thérèse de Parabère
as Minerva: engraving by F. Guibert after Jean-Baptiste Santerre, *c.* 1715

Image: Bibliothèque nationale de France

Quinziéme Ordre

La Régente ou La Minerve

This sombre allemande portrays the other side of the Regent (see *La Coribante, Twelfth Ordre,* and the *Thirteenth Ordre*). Philippe d'Orléans was a highly cultured man, a good musician who studied what was then early music, composed operas and was also a good painter. He was liked and respected by both musicians and artists. Like so many people at the time he was seriously interested in science and tried his hand at experiments himself. He created the official title of *Ordinaire de la Musique du Roi* for Couperin, a post that carried with it a pension. This is the Regent of *La Régente ou La Minerve*, Minerva being the Roman goddess of wisdom and the arts. Couperin's portrait is another example of his evident sympathy for the man.

Le Dodo ou L'amour au Berçeau

The Regent's portrait is followed by a lullaby, *Le Dodo* or Cupid in the cradle, based on the tune *Le Carillon d'Orléans. Dodo* is baby-talk for sleep. *L'Amour au Berceau* appears as a title for paintings. Couperin does not bother with a capital A for *Amour*, which signifies Cupid.

L'evaporée

Still the Regent, in his dissipated, disorganized state. Furetière: 'Se dissiper, se perdre, s'emporter, s'échapper son esprit évaporée' ('To squander, to lose, to fly into a passion, to escape from one's dissipated mind').

Muséte de Choisi

Bagpipes (the bellows-blown musette was the aristocratic bagpipe) were erotic symbols in French art at the time. Choisy was a country house near Paris that belonged to the Conti family. The Regent's mother describes it: 'On Monday I am going to stay with the Prince de Conti at Choisy. It is a beautiful residence, [...] very pleasantly situated on the banks of the Seine and the gardens go so near the river that it is very pleasant to fish there.'[88] It is also likely that there is a double meaning here. The Abbé de Choisy, as Derek Connon explains (pp. 58–9), is a likely candidate. He was a frequent attender at the salon of the Marquise de Lambert, where Couperin played. Madame de Lambert was somewhat sceptical where virtue was concerned and she appreciated the Abbé's knowledge of the world and his amused irony.[89]

Musête de Taverni

One of the Regent's country houses was at Taverny, which was probably the scene of some of his notorious parties.

La Douce et Piquante

Douce, Furetière: 'Paisible, civil, complaisant, rien de rude' ('Quiet, polite, obliging, nothing disagreeable').

Piquante: 'Cette beauté a quelque chose de piquant qui la fait aimer de tout le monde' ('This beauty has something piquant that makes her loved by everyone').

Les Vergers fleüris

Literally, the flowering orchards. Marked *Louré*; *loure* was the name given to the bagpipe in old Normandy. Presumably these are the lutenists and oboe players of the Du Verger family, the first section being in the lute register and the second 'in the style of the *cornemuse*', a mouth-blown bagpipe with a double reed that was played by the upper classes at the time. Furetière: 'Style fleuri, orné' ('Ornate, florid style').

88. Duchesse d'Orléans, *The Letters of Madame*, trans. and ed. Gertrude Scott Stevenson, II, p. 203, 22 April 1719.
89. Glotz and Maire, *Salons*, p. 86.

La Princesse de Chabeüil ou La Muse de Monaco

In a letter to Couperin dated 28 July 1722, Prince Antoine of Monaco, thanking the composer for his daughter's piece, writes: 'She is like a kitten who plays about with the ornaments that bother her.'[90]

Seiziéme Ordre

The architecture of this *ordre* is discussed on p. 101.

Les Graces incomparables ou La Conti

François-Louis de Bourbon, Prince de Conti. Saint Simon describes him:

> There was a grace in everything he did, yet he was wholly unaffected. [...] In appearance he was most pleasing; even the defects of his body and mind had immense charm; his head tilted slightly on one side, his laugh, which in any other would have been called the braying of an ass, his absent-mindedness.[91]

Couperin uses the little figure that opens the second half of this piece to denote the braying of an ass elsewhere (see *Les Chinois, Twenty-seventh Ordre*) and this is what nails this portrait as the Prince rather than the ladies of the family. Conti was brilliant and brave; he treated everyone with equal charm, however lowly they may have been. He was popular, with a great gift for friendship. He was clever, interested in all the arts and sciences, but he could be light-hearted and frivolous with the less serious at court. He was particularly interested in the theatre, of which he was a great patron. *Grâces incomparables* indeed. He had everything, which was his misfortune, because the King resented his superiority over

90. Mellers, *François Couperin,* p. 417.
91. *Saint Simon*, I, p. 420.

his own sons, just as he did with Philippe d'Orléans. His final undoing came when a letter he wrote home from the wars was opened by the King, who found himself referred to as 'The Monarch of the Stage'. Conti was banished to Chantilly.[92] The piece *La Distraite*, which comes later in this *ordre*, could refer to the Prince's absent-mindedness. This radiant allemande is a great contrast to *La Régente* (*Fifteenth Ordre*).

L'Himen-Amour

Conti was in love with his brother-in-law's wife (the Duchesse de Bourbon), an affair that lasted till death parted them, but they conducted it with such discretion that they offended neither his wife nor her husband. There is a play by Regnard's colleague Dufresny called *Les Mal-assortis*:

> Le Théâtre represente la Salle des Mal-assortis. On voit l'Hymen au milieu de quantité de Maris & de Femmes qui se tournent les dos, & qui rechignent l'un contre l'autre. L'Hymen est assis sous un Arbre sec, tout plein d'Oiseaux de mauvais augure, comme Coucous, Hiboux, Chauve-souris, &c. La symphonie joue un air fort triste.[93]

> (The stage represents the Room of the Ill-matched Couples. You see Hymen amongst a number of husbands and wives who turn their backs on each other and who scowl at each other. He is sitting under a dead tree on which perch birds of evil-omen; cuckoos, owls, bats etc. The orchestra plays a sad air.)

Not only does this piece mimic cuckoos (in the bass), owls and bats, but wedding bells are also briefly heard in bar 5. In the play, Arlequin enters with a speech that opens: 'O Hymen, Protecteur du chagrin domestique' ('protector of domestic gloom'), which is followed by Hymen's song:

92. Nancy Mitford, *The Sun King*, p. 119.
93. Dufresny, *Les Mal-assortis*, in Gherardi, *Théâtre italien*, IV, p. 373.

Je sais le malheur extrème,
De la plupart des humains;
Mais leur bonheur suprème
Est aussi dans mes mains.
En ma droite, je tiens l'heureuse destinée;
Ma gauche livre le tourment.
Celle-cy, par malheur, s'ouvre facilement,
Et ma droite est toujours fermée.[94]

(I am aware of the extreme unhappiness of most human beings, but their happiness is also in my hands. In my right hand I hold good fortune, my left releases torment. The latter, sadly, opens easily, but my right is always closed.)

One of Couperin's great preoccupations was with the two sides of everything. The second part of this piece ought to be blissfully happy, with a drone bass – bagpipes were an erotic symbol in French art at the time – however, Couperin has separated the notes in the bass, continuing the irony of the first half.

Les Vestales

One of the pieces that were parodied. These vestal virgins of Couperin's figure in his vocal canon *Les Trois Vestales Champêtres et Les Trois Poliçons* (see pp. 33–4). The canon, like the harpsichord piece, is in two parts, the first mock-innocent and the second voluptuous, to borrow a word used by the composer himself. A *poliçon* was a 'loose person', according to Furetière. He also says of a vestal: 'On dit maintenant, quand on veut adoucir le mot en parlant d'une femme qui ne vit pas fort regulièrement, qu'elle ne se pique pas d'être vestale' ('One says nowadays, when one wants to speak politely of a woman who lives somewhat irregularly, that she doesn't pride herself on being a vestal'). In the first part of the canon the virgins keep mortals away from their pure altars, and in

94. *Les Mal-assortis*, p. 374.

the second we have Louison, Suzon and Thérése (see *L'aimable Thérése*) making love and being paid with *bilboquets*, toys. The reference is to a cup-and-ball game, so there is an erotic connotation.

L'aimable Thérése

Thérèse Lenoir de La Thorillière, 'as celebrated for her beauty as for her talent'.[95] She was 'one of the most fascinating and beautiful women of her time who acted amorous roles in comedies with all the grace and finesse possible'.[96] She enticed the playwright Florent Dancourt (see *La Florentine, Second Ordre*) away from a respectable profession in the law, but sadly they turned out to be another 'ill-matched' couple. Thérèse lived in a smart house in the Bois de Boulogne where, as a poem puts it:

> On di que chez la Dancourt
> On y joue au jeu de l'amour,
>   Ce n'est qu'une médisance;
>   Son carrosse et sa dépense
>   Sont les fruits de sa beauté.[97]

(They say that in Madame Dancourt's house they play the game of love, this is but slander. Her coach and all she spends are the results of her beauty.)

The Dancourts had two actress daughters, Manon and Mimi (see *First* and *Second Ordres*).

Le Drôle de Corps

A reference to the theatre: this is the joker of the troupe. Marked *gaillardement*; Furetière: 'Qui ne demande qu'à rire' ('Who asks only to laugh').

95. Campardon, *Troupe française*, p. 1.
96. Titon Du Tillet, *Le Parnasse françois*, p. 607.
97. Mongrédien, *Daily Life*, p. 205.

La Distraite

Someone absent-minded (see *La Conti* above), or possibly a reference to the Regnard play of that name, which could equally be a portrait of the Prince, since Regnard was a playwright he particularly patronized. Regnard was a favourite of Couperin's as well, and he owned a copy of his plays (see p. 48). It could also be someone distracted by love.

La Létiville

Possibly the Abbé Jacques d'Estival or Destival (? –1733), a tenor who sang in Couperin's motets; one of a dynasty of singers, he held the post of 'taille' at the Royal Chapel, becoming Chapelain du Roi and Prieur de Largeau, and later Chanoine de Saint-Quentin. His brother Guillaume (? –1719) was a 'basse-taille', also at the Chapel Royal. Although probably deriving from the village of Estival in the Auvergne, the name has a built-in double meaning, since *estival*, like English 'aestival', is an adjective relating to summer. If Couperin chose not to exploit this link, it is probably because it was simply too obvious; indeed, perhaps he was aware that, like most people with punnable names, d'Estival was already heartily sick of the joke. Although at first sight 'Létiville' seems very remote from this name, making it, if the identification is correct, one of the most complex pieces of word-play in the *ordres*, it is created by three characteristically Couperinesque steps. First the 'de', the *particule*, is replaced by a definite article, so that the word represents the man himself, not just his place of origin; the lack of an apostrophe is not unusual – the tendency for articles and *particules* to be absorbed into the main body of the name can already be seen in the variant spelling of Destival, perhaps the spelling known to Couperin. The transformation of the 'es' into 'e' acute is a common piece of morphology in the development of French, apparent in the relationship between the etymologically linked pair *estival* and *été*,

where the more learned adjective retains the 's' from the etymo-
logical root, whilst it has disappeared from the more commonly
used noun – it is not impossible that this shift was reflected in the
pronunciation of the name, despite the continued presence of the
's' in its spelling. Finally, the transformation of *val* into *ville* is
similar to the game found in the transformation of Losinthal into
Logiviére, in the *Fifth Ordre*, which also replaces a valley with a
different geographical feature. If the piece does portray one or both
of the singers it seems to be an in-joke, as much of it is not
particularly singable.

Dixseptiéme Ordre

La Superbe ou la Forqueray

Antoine Forqueray, the celebrated viol player and composer who
played with Couperin. *Superbe* can mean proud, which was
certainly true of Forqueray. He was a difficult and pompous man
and this grand, but rather pretentious, and for long stretches
vacuous, allemande must surely indicate that the great viol player
was something of a trial to Couperin. This is another contrast to
the two previous allemandes. In return, Forqueray's own angular
portrait of Couperin is not exactly complimentary. Couperin's viol
pieces are very awkwardly written for the instrument, which may
explain this situation.[98]

Les Petits Moulins à Vent

Windmills, idle chatterboxes. This piece is pompous too, with its
octaves in the bass, and may well refer to Forqueray's empty
conversation. Furetière: 'On dit de toutes les mechantes
comparaisons qu'on veut blâmer, cela ressemble mieux qu'un

98. I am grateful to Laurence Dreyfus for this observation.

moulin à vent' ('One says of all the bad similes one wants to criticize, there is a better resemblance than with a windmill').

Les Timbres

Bells struck by hand with hammers. Also used in the sense 'Il a le timbre fêlé' ('He is a bit cracked'). Furetière: 'Se dit figurement et bassement de la cervelle d'un homme, ou de son esprit. On dit d'un fou, que son timbre n'est pas sain, que son timbre est cassé' ('Used figuratively and commonly of the brain of a man, or of his spirit. One says of a madman that his *timbre* is not sane, that his *timbre* is broken'). The piece probably still refers to Forqueray, who was unstable.

Courante

The only dance movement in *Book III*; it may refer to Forqueray's style.

Les Petites Chrémiéres de Bagnolet

The little dairymaids of Bagnolet. The Duc d'Orléans gave the chateau of Bagnolet to his wife and it became her favourite residence during the Regency. There she and her friends played at being peasants. Presumably the repeated figures in the second half are the cows mooing. Forqueray taught the Regent, so there may be a connection here.

Dixhuitiéme Ordre

Allemande La Verneüil

Achille Varlet, Sieur de Verneuil, actor famous for his tragic roles and head of the King's French troupe, is the most likely candidate, taking the contents of the rest of the *ordre* into account.[99] He was

99. Eugène Despois, *Le Théâtre Français sous Louis XIV*, pp. 17, 38, 51.

the brother of Charles Varlet, Sieur de La Grange, who had worked with Molière and in 1680 became the first administrator of the Comédie Française. Achille also joined the company. Their father was Procurateur du Roi in Montpellier. This magnificent allemande (see p. 100) has nothing of the empty pomposity of *La Forqueray* in the *Seventeenth Ordre*.

La Verneüilléte

Marie Vallée, actress wife of Verneuil. They had two sons, one of whom became an attorney in the Parlement de Paris and the other a distinguished missionary.

Sœur Monique

Also parodied (see p. 34 and *Les Vestales*, *Sixteenth Ordre*). The word *sœur* (sister) was used ironically to mean girls of ill repute. Furetière: 'On dit proverbialement et ironiquement, Voilà de nos sœurs, pour dire des coureuses, des filles débauchees' ('One says ironically and proverbially, there are our sisters, meaning street-walkers, debauched girls'). Like *Les Vestales*, this piece had two distinct faces, mock-innocent in the *rondeau* and seductive, as indicated by the markings, in the *couplets*.

Le Turbulent

Furetière: 'Qui est violent, remuant, impetueux; qui est porté de faire du bruit, du désordre' ('One who is violent, disturbing, impetuous; who is given to making a stir, confusion').

L'atendrissante

Furetière: 'Mouvement du cœur qui lui fait concevoir de la tendresse, de l'amitié, de la compassion pour quelqu'un' ('Something that makes the heart feel tenderness, affection, compassion for someone'). So repetitive, it could be ironic.

Le Tic-Toc-Choc ou les Maillotins

There was a famous family of rope-dancers at the Fair theatres called Maillot. Furetière: 'Tic toc; un terme indeclinable et factice, qui exprime un battement, un mouvement reiteré, un pouls qui bat, un cheval qui marche, une balance d'orloge, un marteau qui frappe' ('An indeclinable and artificial term, which expresses a beating, a reiterated movement, a pulse that beats, a horse that walks, the pendulum of a clock, a hammer that knocks'). It also describes the movements of a rope-dancer: 'The strapados and the oscillations that they make on the ropes make the spectators' hair stand on end.'[100] (*Concise Oxford Dictionary*: 'Strapado, torture inflicted by securing person's hands or other part in ropes, raising him and letting him fall till brought up by taut rope. Oscillation, swing like a pendulum.') The rope-dancers' hands were often occupied in playing the violin, frequently behind their backs or over their heads.

Le Gaillard-Boiteux

Marked to be played 'dans le Goût Burlesque', which refers to the Italian comedy. Furetière: 'Burlesque, ce mot est assez moderne. [...] Il nous est venu d'Italie. Il ne regna pas longtemps, à cause qu'on y introduit trop de licence, et trop de ridicules plaisanteries' ('This word is quite modern. [...] It came to us from Italy. It was not in fashion for long because they [the Italian actors] introduced too much licence and too many ridiculous jokes').

One of the dancing masters at Versailles was called Jean Gaillard. In Regnard and Dufresny's play *Les Chinois* (see the *Twenty-seventh Ordre*), we are told that the actors are going to mock themselves at last, having mocked everyone else: 'Il n'y a point de profession qui ait échappé à leur Satire; Procureurs,

---

100. Nemeitz, *Séjour*, p. 109.

Medecins, Magistrats. [...] Ils n'ont pas mesme respecté les Empereurs Romains, ny les Maistres à Danser'[101] ('There is not a profession that has escaped their satire; Attorneys, Doctors, Magistrates. [...] They have not even respected Roman Emperors or dancing masters'). In the scene in question, from Boisfran's *Arlequin misanthrope*, the dancing master, Mr. de Colafon, has a wooden leg; *boiteux* means lame.

> ARLEQUIN: Et quelle est votre profession?
> COLAFON: J'étois Maitre à Danser à l'Opera de Lyon, mais comme l'Opera est tombé...
> ARLEQUIN: Il vous est tombé sur le corps, & vous voila tout estropié?[102]
>
> (HARLEQUIN: And what is your profession?
> COLAFON: I was the dancing master at the opera house in Lyon, but as the opera has fallen...
> HARLEQUIN: It fell on you I suppose, and there you are, completely crippled?)

For some reason Gaillard was the object of both Boisfran's and Couperin's wit. There is also the play on his name: Furetière defines a *gaillard* as a person who 'ne demande qu'à rire' ('asks only to laugh').

Dixneuviéme Ordre

Les Calotins et les Calotines ou la Piéce à tretous
Le Régiment de la Calotte was a French play performed at the Fair theatres in 1721 (see p. 89). The *dramatis personae* include a 'Troupe de Calotins et de Calotines'. It was a comedy about a

---

101. Regnard and Dufresny, *Les Chinois*, in Gherardi, *Théâtre italien*, IV, p. 216.
102. Boisfran, *Arlequin misanthrope*, in Gherardi, *Théâtre italien*, VI, p. 543.

spoof regiment founded in 1702 by some bored wags at Versailles, who enlisted anyone, from any rank, who distinguished themselves by a ridiculous trait, a squint or a limp or a twitch. When someone asked Louis XIV why he never brought the regiment out on parade he said there would be no one left to inspect it. The play alludes to contemporary personalities and events. The first Calotin is a lawyer whose folly consists not only of marrying a woman who subsequently cuckolds him but who, in taking her to court about it, lets everyone else know what she has done to him. In recognition of his stupidity Momus (god of folly) appoints him trumpeter in the Brigade of Cuckolds.[103] The trumpet appears in bars 29–33 and the cuckoos in bars 39–41 of *Les Calotines*. Furetière: 'Calotte, petit bonnet de cuir, de satin ou autre étoffe, qui couvre le haut de la tête. Il n'y a gueres que les vieillards qui portent les calottes' ('Little cap of leather or satin or other material, which covers the top of the head. It is really only old people who wear *calottes*'). *Tretou* is generally accepted to mean *tréteau*, trestle (stage), but, as Derek Connon points out (p. 86), trestles had long since ceased to be used by the main theatrical companies at the Fairs by this time. However, it is possible that the Fair plays were always referred to in this way. Another explanation is given by Furetière: 'Tréteau, on dit d'un mechant boufon ou un mechant comedien, Il n'est bon qu'à monter sur les trétaux' ('One says of a bad clown or a bad actor, he is only good enough for the trestles'). This is perhaps the correct implication in this case, since the play mocks the Nouveau Théâtre Italien, the troupe the Regent patronized and which opened in 1716. It is likely that Couperin would compare the new Italian actors unfavourably to Gherardi's

---

103. Lesage and d'Orneval, *Le Théâtre de la Foire*, V, p. 24. I am grateful to Derek Connon for this reference.

original troupe. In the final scene of *Le Régiment de la Calotte*, which opens with a 'mad march', the new Italian actors are welcomed into the regiment. As is usual in the Lesage and d'Orneval anthology, the vocal music is preserved, but not the purely instrumental numbers. However, since we know the vaudeville finale to be by Aubert, and since no other instance of Couperin contributing music to the Fair theatres has come down to us, it is perhaps unlikely that his *Pièce à tretous* was incidental music but rather a humorous amalgam of the incidents he presumably enjoyed most, opening with the 'mad march'.

L'ingénuë

In another of Regnard's plays, *La Foire Saint Germain*, an *ingénue* (naïve girl) comes to consult the Mouth of Truth. She wants to know if she is to be married this year. Arlequin tells her to put her hand in the mouth and swear she is a virgin. After a lot of banter she says: 'Je suis très humble servante à la Bouche de la Verité, mais j'ay trop peur de ses vilaines dents-là'[104] ('Much as I respect your Mouth of Truth, I'm too scared of his nasty teeth'). Yet another piece with two sides.

L'Artiste

A bonnet.[105] The serene beauty of its wearer is a contrast to the tongue-in-cheek *ingénue*.

Les Culbutes Ixcxbxnxs

A *culbute* is a somersault, most commonly a somersault done in bed. There is no reason to suppose that, as has sometimes been suggested, *Ixcxbxnxs* refers to Jacobites, who were one of the few

104. Regnard and Dufresny, *La Foire Saint Germain*, in Gherardi, *Théâtre italien*, VI, p. 246.
105. Franklin, *La Vie privée*, XVIII, *Les Magasins*, III, p. 247.

communities whose morals seem to have escaped satire. *Jacobins* is the familiar term for the Dominican order of monks and nuns, who may have had particularly lax morals, since they appear in satirical verses in affairs with both boys and women. One is 'Sur plusieurs dames qui alloient à la messe des Jacobins de la rue Saint Honoré':

> Dans ce temple jadis si saint,
> Si quelque Dieu est encort craint,
> Ce n'est plus celui de nos pères.
> Laire la, laire……..
>
> L'enfant que l'on y adoroit,
> La mère qu'on y respectoit,
> Ont fait place aux dieux de Cithère,
> Laire la, laire……..[106]

(In this temple formerly so holy, if any God is still feared, it is not that of our fathers. The child that was adored here, the mother whom they respected, have been replaced by gods of love.)

Furetière: 'On ne se sert du mot de Jacobins que dans le style familier, car dans le style grave on dit Dominicains' ('One only uses the word Jacobins in the familiar style, for in a serious style one says Dominicans'). And of *culbutes* he says: 'Chûtes morales' ('Moral downfalls').

La Muse-Plantine

Mademoiselle de La Plante, a harpsichordist and composer, who combined 'La delicatesse et le brilliant de toucher à une science parfaite de la composition'[107] ('A delicacy and brilliance in playing with a perfect knowledge of composition').

106. Maurepas, *Recueil*, II, p. 359.
107. Titon Du Tillet, *Le Parnasse françois*, p. 637.

L'enjouée

A *mouche* (patch) worn in the crease of the cheek made by laughing.[108] Furetière claims that if used as a noun *enjoué* can only mean a *mouche*.

BOOK IV (1730)

Vingtiéme Ordre

La Princesse Marie

Polish fiancée of Louis XV, hence the last section *Air dans le goût Polonois*. The princess, who had a sweet nature and a regal manner, was a pupil of Couperin: 'S'applicant beaucoup a ses exercices, Mr. Couperin luy montre à jouer du clavecin et Mouret de chez Madame Dumaine la musique'[109] ('Applying herself well to her studies, Mr. Couperin teaches her the harpsichord and Mouret, from the household of Madame Du Maine, music theory').

An old court dance, the polonaise is said to have derived from court processions in the late sixteenth century. In moderate triple time it is a rhythmic processional march with emphasis on the second beat. It was led by the most important person present, with flourishes, bows and dignified movements. It was danced originally only by men as a dance of knighthood. At appropriate moments they swept off their plumed hats or, with a flourish, drew their swords from their scabbards. This dignified dance of rigid eti-

108. Franklin, *La Vie privée*, II, *Les Soins de la Toilette*, p. 96.

109. From a letter of 16 June 1724 from Louis Langers to Jean Delamare quoted in Norbert Dufourcq and Marcelle Benoit, 'La vie musicale en Île de France sous la Régence: douze années à la Chapelle Royale de Musique d'après une correspondance inédite (1716–1728)', p. 161.

quette spread in the eighteenth century, and was probably danced by the Poles who delivered the princess to the French court. Couperin's stiff and somewhat exaggerated version perhaps betrays the fact that, in contrast to the charming sincerity of the young princess, he found the eastern European etiquette slightly ridiculous (see p. 50).

La Boufonne

A theatrical reference, this is a real joker, bringing the *ordre* down to earth. Furetière: 'Mime ou Pantomime. Farceur qui fait mille grimaces, mille postures, et dit mille folies ou mille sottises pour faire rire les gens. Les comediens Italiens sont les meilleurs Bouffons' ('Practical joker who pulls a thousand faces, does a thousand acrobatic tricks,[110] and says a thousand mad things, a thousand silly things in order to make people laugh. The Italian actors are the best clowns'). Marked *gaillardement*, with a laugh.

Les Chérubins ou L'aimable Lazure

A 'cherubin' is a blushing but willing maid. Furetière: 'On dit d'une personne haute en couleur, ou qui rougit de honte, elle est rouge comme un cherubin' ('One says of someone who has a high colour, or who blushes from shame, she is red like a cherub'). This may be a reference to one of the celebrated Loyson sisters (see *Les Nonètes, First Ordre*, and *Les Juméles, Twelfth Ordre*), Doguine, who, in her portrait (see p. 51), is shown with a flirtatious and scantily clad Cupid on her knee; cherubs, *putti* and Cupids in art are often confused. She is wearing blue (*azure*) and is surrounded by doves, symbols of purity. Her lifestyle did not warrant this image.

---

110. A *posture* was any sort of acrobatic routine which required a pose to be held to make its effect, as for instance a handstand or a human pyramid.

La Croûilli ou la Couperinéte

Presumably Couperin's daughter, Marguerite-Antoinette, who in 1730 became *Ordinaire de la chambre pour le clavecin* at the court of Louis XV in place of her father, who was sometimes referred to as Sieur de Crouilly. Crouilly is the village in Brie where the Couperin family came from. She was a brilliant harpsichordist, whose 'mains enchanteresses' ('enchanted hands') inspired a long poem[111]; she perhaps inspired amorous desires as well, since the piece has a *musette* section. It also bears a resemblance to *L'aimable Thérése* (see *Sixteenth Ordre*).

La Fine Madelon
La Douce Janneton

Jeanne de Beauval, always known as Jeanneton, in her celebrated role as Madelon in Molière's *Les Précieuses ridicules*. This little prig, on her father's mention of marriage, quotes *La Carte de Tendre* (see *Les Langueurs-Tendres, Sixth Ordre*) at him, upon which the poor man remarks: 'Quel diable de jargon entends-je? Voici bien du haut style.' Madelon reproaches him with: 'Mon Dieu! Que vous êtes vulgaire! Pour moi, un de mes étonnements, c'est que vous ayez pu faire une fille si spirituelle que moi'[112] ('What devil of a jargon do I hear? Here's fine style.' Madelon: 'My God, you are vulgar, I am astonished that you have been able to produce such a witty and intellectual daughter as I am'). Couperin's marking *affectueusement* must be ironic (see *La Flateuse, Second Ordre*).

In *La Douce Janneton*, marked *plus voluptueusement*, we have the actress herself. Jeanneton appears with Fanchon in the canon 'Woman between two Sheets' (see p. 33), and history credits her with twenty-eight children.

---

111. Quoted in full in Charles Bouvet, *Les Couperins*, pp. 117–18.
112. Scene iv.

La Sézile

Nicolas Sézile, Trésorier des Offrandes et Aumônes du Roi. *Gracieusement* here almost certainly refers to *grâces* in the sense of 'favours' (see *L'Etincelante ou La Bontems, Eleventh Ordre*). A grand and masculine piece in contrast to the previous portrait. The short phrases are presumably the charitable gifts being handed out.

Les Tambourins

The *tambourin* is said to be based on a Provençal folkdance accompanied by pipe and tabor. The bass represents the drum and the upper voice the pipe. The dance was much used in the theatre.

Vingt-Uniéme Ordre

La Reine des cœurs

Furetière: 'Maitresse qui domine, qui a un grand pouvoir' ('A mistress who dominates, who has great power').

La Bondissante

Possibly a bounding heart, or it could have the same meaning as the canon *La Femme entre deux Draps* (see p. 33) and *La Fringante* (*Tenth Ordre*) and refer to bounding horses (women) who give you a rough ride.

La Couperin

The composer himself. Dagincour's wonderful portrait of Couperin is also an allemande in E minor. Dagincour was a self-confessed disciple of Couperin and his piece is worthy of its subject. Couperin harks back to *La Bondissante* in his allemande. The figure in bars 5, 7 and 8 refers to the figure that first appears in bar 4 and, most important, in bar 23, at the end of the previous piece.

La Harpée, Pièce dans le goût de la Harpe

Several meanings can be given to this title and probably Couperin is playing on them all. It is a bombastic piece in contrast to the introspective *Couperin*. Furetière: 'Harper, se quereller, se prendre au collet, aux cheveux' ('To quarrel, to seize by the scruff of the neck, by the hair'). 'Ces deux femmes se sont harpées après s'être dit beaucoup d'injures' ('These two women have quarrelled after they have insulted one another'). Perhaps a mistress who had quarrelled with Couperin is the most probable meaning. Alternatively someone who had stolen his mistress. Furetière: 'On dit proverbialement et bassement, pour taxer un homme d'être voleur, qu'il est parent du Roi David, qu'il joue de la Harpe' ('They say proverbially and vulgarly when charging a man with being a robber, that he is a kinsman of King David, that he plays the harp').

> HARLEQUIN en Vicomte à Colombine: Vous sçaurez donc, qu'estant obligé de partir pour l'Allemagne, & ne pouvant trouver d'argent sur mon Billet, car les Billets des Vicomtes ne sont pas autrement reputez argent comptant, j'en fis un que je signay La Harpe, c'est le nom de ce fameux Banquier. Sur ce Billet-là on me donna deux cent pistoles. Je partis. Presentement, voyez je vous prie, le peu de bonne foy qu'il y a dans le Commerce! ce vilain Monsieur de la Harpe ne veut pas payer ce Billet-là.[113]

> (HARLEQUIN as a Viscount to Columbine: You know of course that, being obliged to leave for Germany, and not being able to get any money on my promissory note, for the notes of Viscounts are not considered ready money, I made one that I signed La Harpe, this is the name of the famous banker. On this note they gave me two hundred *pistoles*. I left. Now, you see what little honour there is in commerce! this wicked Monsieur de La Harpe does not want to pay up.)

113. Regnard, *L'Homme à bonne fortune*, in Gherardi, *Théâtre italien*, II, p. 497.

La Petite Pince-sans-rire
Sly or malicious remark. Furetière: 'Il pince sans rire, sans en faire semblant, il dit les veritez de chacun' ('Without appearing to he speaks the truth about each one'). Marked *affectueusement*, again surely ironic.

This and the next *ordre* seem to tell the story of love affairs that went wrong. This *ordre* is sad and bitter, perhaps Couperin's own experience, and the next humorous.

Vingt-Deuxiéme Ordre

Le Trophée
Premier Air pour la suite du Trophée
Probably originally theatre music, reminiscent of Lully. An amorous trophy (see *Le Bavolet-flotant, Ninth Ordre*) is followed by an amorous air.

Le point du jour, Allemande
Daybreak. The morning after catching the amorous trophy?

L'Anguille
The eel, some slippery character. Furetière: 'Il y a anguille sous roche; pour dire il y a quelque mystère caché, sous ce qu'il dit, ou sous ce qu'il fait' ('There is an eel under the rock; meaning there is some hidden mystery beneath what someone says or what he does'). Today this might be translated as 'something fishy'. A devious lover? *Matelote d'Anguille* was a hornpipe.

Le Croc-en-jambe
To trip someone up, a common term in burlesque plays. Furetière: 'Un tour d'adresse de ceux qui ruinent un projet, une affaire, la fortune de leur ennemi, qui supplante son rival. Il a donnée croc-en-jambe à Cupidon' ('Trickery of those who ruin a project, an

affair, the fortune of their enemy, who supplant a rival. He has tripped up Cupid [i.e. deceived someone in love]').

Menuets croisés

One hand on each keyboard. An amorous duet?

Les Tours de Passe-passe

Conjuring tricks, sleight of hand, trickery. Furetière: 'Les subtilitez que font les Charlatans pour se faire admirer par le peuple, ou pour s'amuser, ou l'attraper' ('The craft of a charlatan to make people admire him, or to amuse himself, or to trap them'). Perhaps finally the deceived lover is on his own with his hands crossed on one keyboard (a technique Rameau claimed to have invented).

Vingt-Troisiéme Ordre

L'Audacieuse

A reference to the début of the Arlequin Evaristo Gherardi. He first appeared in Regnard's *Le Divorce*, playing a part in which his legendary predecessor Biancolelli had failed. Because Gherardi dared to take over the role, in which he had an immediate success, his début was known as *la tentative audacieuse*. The stage directions say he has to enter 'en colère', angry. To the troupe:

> He que diable, Messieurs, ne sçauriez-vous mieux prendre votre temps pour estre malades? Cela est de la derniere impertinence, de se trouver mal quand il faut gagner de l'argent. Que voulez-vous que je fasse de tout ce monde-là?

> (The devil take you, gentlemen, don't you know any better than to take time off being ill? That's the last straw, to be ill when it's necessary to earn some money. What do you think I'm going to do with all those people?)

Evaristo Gherardi as Arlequin:
engraving by P. J. Mariette

Image: Bibliothèque nationale de France

To the audience:

Messieurs, ce que je vais vous dire vous déplaira peut-estre; mais en
vérité j'en suis plus fâché que vous, & personne n'y perd tant que
moy. Nous ne pouvons pas jouer la Comedie aujourd'huy; voila
notre Portier qui vient de se trouver mal, & Pantalon qui devoit faire
un rolle de Patrocle, est indisposé. On va vous rendre votre argent
à la porte. Vous voyez, Messieurs, que nous ne suivons pas les
mauvais exemples, & que nous rendons l'argent, quoy que la
Comedie soit commencée.[114]

(Gentlemen, what I have to say to you will perhaps displease you, but
in truth I am more angry than you are, and no one stands to lose as
much as me. We cannot play the comedy today; there is our janitor
who has just had a turn, and Pantalon who ought to play the role of
Patroclus is indisposed. We will give you your money back at the
door. You see, gentlemen, we don't follow bad examples, we give
back the money even though the comedy has begun.)

Les Tricoteuses

The most obvious meaning is the knitters with their *mailles-lâchées*
(dropped stitches) in bars 38–40. However, a *tricoteur* was also a
chicaneur (someone who tries to catch people out, rascally
attorney) or *tracasseur* (busybody, mischief-maker, troublesome
person).[115] An element of this meaning must be intended, since
trickery raises its head so often in these last *ordres*. For such a good-
natured piece it must be the trickery of the *commedia* rather than
any bitter experience Couperin suffered.

L'Arlequine

Marked *grotesquement*; Furetière: 'Bizarre, extravagant, plaisam-
ment ridicule' ('Odd, eccentric, amusingly ridiculous'). The
strange jerkiness describes the movements of a harlequin exactly. It

114. Regnard, *Le Divorce*, in Gherardi, *Théâtre italien*, II, p. 109.
115. *Dictionnaire de la langue française du seizième siècle.*

is a grotesque chaconne; the music of some of Arlequin's chaconnes survives.[116] The very fact that Arlequin was performing an aristocratic dance like the chaconne would be grotesque in itself. By his markings Couperin has distorted the dance rhythm. It is possible that at the beginning he is imitating a fairground organ, remembering that Gherardi's plays were done at the Fair theatres.

This can certainly be read as an agonizingly nostalgic piece, in the mood of the great French cabaret singers of the twentieth century; Couperin simply got there first.

The passage of discords at bars 24–31 may be inspired by a scene from *Le Divorce* (see *L'Audacieuse* above) in which Arlequin is singing a duet with Mezzetin, an Italian singing master. Arlequin's efforts are not a great success and Mezzetin, driven mad, pleads: 'Chantez donc juste si vous voulez.' Arlequin, who insists he is an accomplished musician, retorts: 'Oh, chantez juste, vous mesme; je sçay bien ce que je dis. Est-ce que je ne vois pas bien qu'il faut marquer là une dissonance, & que l'octave s'entre-choquant avec l'unisson, vient à former un Diesis b mol.'[117] (Mezzetin: 'Do please sing in tune.' Arlequin: 'Oh, sing in tune yourself; I know what I'm talking about. Do you think I don't know perfectly well that it's necessary to mark a dissonance there, and that the octave comes in clashing with the unison, forming a B sharp minor?')

Les Gondoles de Délos

Louis XIV was presented with gondolas by the Venetians. They were used on the lake at Versailles. In mythology Delos is the birthplace of Apollo, god of music and poetry. The title could refer to a *divertissement* in which gondolas had figured on the lake. They also appear in plays:

116. *The New Grove Dictionary of Music & Musicians*, IV, p. 101.
117. Regnard, *Le Divorce*, in Gherardi, *Théâtre italien*, II, p. 148.

Le Théâtre represente une Rivière. On voit La Verité dans une magnifique Gondole, qui avance jusqu'au bord du Théâtre, au son des instruments.[118]

(The stage represents a river. You see Truth in a magnificent gondola, which advances towards the edge of the stage, to the sound of instruments.)

Les Satires, Chevre-pieds

Libertines who carried off women. They appear in comedies and paintings of mythical scenes. The second section of the piece is marked *dans un goût burlesque* (see *Le Gaillard-Boiteux, Eighteenth Ordre*). Furetière: 'On dit d'un homme laid et barbu qui est fort adonné aux femmes' ('Said of an ugly and bearded man who is much addicted to women'). 'Chêvre-pied; un épithete que les anciens Poetes donnoient aux Faunes, et aux Satyres, à qui ils attribuoient des pieds de chêvre' ('An epithet that the ancient poets gave to Fauns and Satyrs, to whom they attributed goats' feet').

Vingt-Quatriéme Ordre

The architecture of this *ordre* is discussed on p. 99.

Les Vieux Seigneurs, Sarabande grave
Les Jeunes Seigneurs, Cy-devant les petits Maitres

Les Amusemens sérieux et comiques, a prose piece by Dufresny that was included in the 1721 edition of Gherardi's *Théâtre*, seems to be the idea behind *Les Vieux Seigneurs* and *Les Jeunes Seigneurs, Cy devant les petits Maitres*, or fops. Dufresny says:

---

118. Dufresny and Boisfran, *Pasquin et Marforio*, in Gherardi, *Théâtre italien*, VI, p. 613.

Nymphs and satyrs: engraving by G. Huquier after
Antoine Watteau

Le Courtisan s'étudie à cacher son déréglement sous les dehors réglez. Le Petit Maître fait vanité de paroître encore plus déréglé qu'il n'est. L'un pense beaucoup avant que de parler, l'autre parle beaucoup et ne pense guères. L'un court après la fortune, l'autre croit que la fortune doit courir après lui. Les Courtisans caressent ceux qu'ils méprisent, leurs embrassades servent à cacher leur mépris, quelle dissimulation. Les Petits Maîtres sont plus sincères; ils cachent ni leur amitié, ni leur mépris: la manière dont ils vous abordent tient de l'un et de l'autre, et leurs embrassades sont ordinairement moitié caresses, moitié coups de poing. Le langage courtisan est uniforme, toujours poli, flateur, insinuant; le langage Petit Maître est haut et bas, mêlé de sublime et de trivial, de politesse et de grossiéreté.[119]

(The courtier makes a point of hiding his disorderliness under an orderly exterior, the *petit maître* takes a pride in appearing more disordered than he, in fact, is. One thinks carefully before he speaks, the other talks a lot and scarcely thinks at all. One chases fortune, the other believes that fortune ought to chase him. The courtiers flatter those they scorn, their flatteries serve to hide their scorn, what dissimulation. The *petits maîtres* are more sincere, they hide neither their friendship nor their scorn. The manner in which they approach you is a mixture of both, their attentions are usually half flatteries and half fisticuffs. The courtier's speech is uniform, always polite, flattering, never direct; the speech of the *petit maître* is high and low, a mixture of the sublime and the trivial, of civility and coarseness.)

Les Dars-homicides

Cupid's fatal darts, or fatal glances. Furetière: 'Les amants se plaignent des yeux homicides de leurs maitresses' ('Lovers complain of the fatal eyes of their mistresses').

119. A slightly different version of the text is given in Charles Dufresny, *Les Amusements sérieux et comiques* (Paris: Bossard, 1921). This edition includes an interesting introduction and notes by Jean Vic.

Les Guirlandes

The garlands. Garlands could have erotic connotations. Marked *amoureusement*, it is presumably the result of Cupid's darts.

Les Brinborions

Furetière: 'Terme de mépris, qui sert à exprimer des curiosités légères' ('Scornful term that is used to express trifling curiosities'). Madelon's long-suffering father in Molière's *Les Précieuses ridicules* (see *La Fine Madelon, Twentieth Ordre*) exclaims:

> Ces pendardes-là, avec leur pommade, ont, je pense, envie de me ruiner. Je ne vois partout que blancs d'œufs, lait virginal, et mille autres brimborions que je ne connais point. Elles ont usé, depuis que nous sommes ici, le lard d'une douzaine de cochons pour le moins; et quatre valets vivraient tous les jours des pieds de mouton qu'elles emploient.[120]

> (These jades [that is, Madelon and her cousin], with their pomade, want to ruin me. Everywhere I see whites of egg, virgin milk, and a thousand other *brimborions* that I don't recognize. They have used, since we've been here, the lard of at least a dozen pigs, and four valets would live every day on the sheep's feet they've used.)

One of the longest of the pieces; it shares this distinction with *Les Agrémens* (see *Fifth Ordre*). The aria 'Myself I shall adore' in Handel's *Semele*, sung by Semele as she admires herself in the mirror, is also very long.

La Divine-Babiche ou les amours badins

The lap-dog or playful love. Furetière: 'Badin, peu sérieux' ('Playful'). 'Babiche, vouz perdez pour Babiche des pleurs qui suffiroient pour racheter un Roi' ('You shed for Babiche tears that would serve to redeem a king'). Ironically marked *voluptueusement*.

120. Scene iii.

Burlesque plays often ridiculed the way aristocratic women drooled over their pets.

La belle Javotte autre fois L'Infante

Couperin taught the seven-year-old Infanta of Spain on her ill-fated visit to Paris as prospective bride for Louis XV. Of her entry into Paris the Duchesse d'Orléans writes:

> I can't admire the little Infanta's patience enough, for the poor baby was in that coach for seven hours without crying or getting ill-tempered. She must be the best child in the world, a really good child. That is what she called out to the officer of the bodyguard: 'Ah ne battes ces pauvres gens qui me veulent voir.' ('Don't beat these poor people who want to see me.').[121]

Furetière: 'Javotte, nom de petite fille. Il ne se donne qu'à des filles de basse condition' ('Name for a little girl. Only given to girls of low rank'). *La belle Javotte* is almost certainly a vaudeville. As Derek Connon explains, these tunes were used for different situations and changed their mood accordingly, thus showing that this piece is like the next, amphibious, but its 'noble simplicity' (see *First Ordre, Gavotte*) is in direct contrast to the innuendos of *L'Amphibie*.

L'Amphibie, Mouvement de Passacaille

A speech from Boisfran's play *Les Bains de la Porte Saint Bernard* describes the Amphibian. The scene is a group of *lutins* (sprites; see *La Lutine, Third Ordre*), one of which is strangely clothed. Arlequin is asked about this:

> C'est un Lutin Amphibie, c'est le Lutin qui invente les modes, & qui établie les manieres du monde. Il a l'esprit aussi irregulier que sa figure; il ne laisse rien dans sa simplicité naturelle, & il emprunte toujours quelque chose d'étrange. C'est luy qui fait, par exemple, que

121. *Letters from Liselotte*, p. 239, 5 March 1722.

les jeunes gens du bel air sont par les plaisirs, par les mines, par les promenades, par les mouches, & par les manieres, moins hommes, que femmes; & que les femmes, pour avoir quelque chose de masculin, portent au lieu de Cravattes des Steinquerques, & le poignard au bout; qu'elles fouettent les bouteilles de vin comme les Suisses, le ratafia, & l'eau clairette comme les jeunes Officiers; qu'elles prennent du tabac en poudre comme des Espagnols, & que dans peu elles fumeront comme les Suisses. C'est luy qui en faveur des jeunes Magistrats, a inventé les Rabats en Cravattes, qui n'estant ny l'un ny l'autre, sont pourtant en mesme temps tous les deux, & leur donne un air plus revolté. C'est luy qui a inventé les Papouches, les Perruques à l'Espagnole, qui ne sont ny cheveux naturels ny Perruques, & qui sont en mesme temps & l'un & l'autre. C'est luy enfin qui fait que certaines filles ne sont ny filles ny femmes, & qu'elles sont en mesmes temps toutes les deux.[122]

(That is the *Lutin Amphibie* who invents fashions and who establishes the manners of the world. He has a spirit as strange as his form; he leaves nothing in its natural state. It is he who, for example, ordains that the young men of fashion are by pleasures, by appearances, by gait, by patches and by manners made less men than women, and that women in order to give a masculine impression wear Steinkerques and daggers, that they swallow bottles of wine like the Swiss, Ratafia and *eau clairette* [an *eau-de-vie* made from the *clairette* grape] like young officers, that they take snuff like Spaniards and that shortly they will smoke like the Swiss. It is he who on behalf of young Magistrates has invented the tie-cum-dog-collar (*jabot*) which being neither the one nor the other is at the same time both and gives an air more shocking. It is he who has invented *Papouches* and *Perruques à l'Espagnole*, which being neither natural hair nor wigs are at the same time the one and the other. It is he, finally, who ordains that certain girls are neither girls nor women and that they are at the same time both.)

122. Boisfran, *Les Bains de la Porte Saint Bernard*, in Gherardi, *Théâtre italien*, VI, p. 399.

Alexander Pope was far more scathing in his portrait of the courtier Lord Hervey (see p. 100 above):

> Amphibious thing!
> That acting either part,
> The trifling head, or the corrupted heart
> Fop at the toilet, flatterer at the board,
> Now trips a lady, and now struts a Lord.

Epistle to Dr. Arbuthnot (1735)

La Bruyère also used the term to describe the ambitious courtier in his *Caractères*, a copy of which Couperin possessed (see p. 22). The ambiguity is reflected throughout the piece. As so often with Couperin, *affectueusement*, which is marked for one section of *L'Amphibie*, appears to be ironic.

Vingt-Cinquiéme Ordre

La Visionaire

A play by Desmarets de Saint-Sorlin (see p. 76), performed when Couperin, under an Italian anagram of his name, wrote his early sonatas, one of which is called *La Visionaire*. The last performance of the play was in 1695. This piece, in the Masonic key of E flat, may have some connection with early Freemasonry, which was particularly associated with the Stuart exiles at Saint-Germain (see p. 93 in the essay on Architecture above). The three opening chords and the groups of three notes reinforce this possibility (see *Les Baricades Mistérieuses*, *Sixth Ordre*, and the next piece in this *ordre*). Descartes referred to the Rosicrucians (a type of Freemason) as 'visionnaires'.[123] For Desmarets, as Derek Connon points out (p. 76), *visionnaires* were fantasists. Descartes was

123. Adrien Baillet, *La Vie de Monsieur Descartes*, pp. 106–8.

trying to distance himself from the Brotherhood, so it is hardly surprising that he should have referred to Masons in this way. It is possible that this piece with its two sections, the one grand and dignified and the other fast and crazy, expresses the two images of Masonry: solemn ritual to an initiate and fantastical nonsense to a denigrator. The present Grand Lodge of France believes Couperin to have been a Mason.

The word *visionnaire* is used, with Masonic overtones, in Regnard and Dufresny's play *La Foire Saint Germain*:

> ARLEQUIN: J'ay une fille qui esté serin de Canarie autrefois.
> MEZZETIN: Serin de Canarie? Vous vous moquez Monsieur.
> ARLEQUIN: Non te dis je, Pithagore luy a revelé cela, & elle le croit, c'est sa folie, tu vas voir. (Vers Colombine) Parlez, n'est il pas vray, belle Visionnaire?[124]

> (HARLEQUIN: I have a girl here who was a canary in times gone by.
> MEZZETIN: A canary? You must be joking.
> HARLEQUIN: No, I'm telling you, Pythagoras revealed it to her, and she believes it, it's her fantasy, you'll see. (To Colombine) Tell us, is it not true, pretty Visionnaire?)

La Misterieuse

May also refer to Freemasonry; the groups of three notes reinforce this possibility (see *Les Baricades Mistérieuses*, *Sixth Ordre*, and the first piece in this *ordre*). Furetière: 'Dogme mysterieux. Les figures de l'Ancien Testament sont mysterieuses. Les anciens Egyptiens ont enveloppé les secrets de leur Religion et de leur Morale sous des caractères mysterieux' ('Mysterious dogma. The figures of the Old Testament are mysterious. The ancient Egyptians enveloped

---

124. Regnard and Dufresny, *La Foire Saint Germain*, in Gherardi, *Théâtre italien*, VI, p. 309.

the secrets of their religion and of their moral philosophy in mysterious characters').

La Montflambert

François Fagnier, Sieur de Monflambert, was councillor at the Châtelet (the criminal courts). He was probably a Freemason. Either he was, despite his position, a gentle and sensitive man, or this is a portrait of his wife.

La Muse Victorieuse

Who this Muse is and why she is victorious is a mystery.

Les Ombres Errantes

As a phrase, lost souls, the shades in Greek mythology who could not descend into Hades because they had not received a proper burial ritual. Couperin could here be thinking of all his theatrical friends and colleagues who had not been able to receive Christian burial. The only way in which anyone connected with the theatre could be given a proper burial ritual was by a written renunciation of their profession. Some were unwilling to comply, and others, like Molière and Gherardi, who died suddenly, were unable to. *Ombres*, spirits of the underworld, are present in many plays. Furetière: 'Un homme vit dans l'ombre, dans l'obscurité, une vie cachée, il mène une vie cachée. Parmi les Epicureans les uns philosophoient à l'ombre, et cachoient leur vie selon le precepte de Pythagore' ('A man lives in shadow, in darkness, a hidden life, he leads a hidden life. Among the Epicureans some philosophized in darkness, and concealed their life according to the precept of Pythagoras'). 'Errantes, les Planetes sont des étoiles errantes. Au lieu que les Planetes parcourent le Zodiaque Pythagore etc. furent si eperdus de la Magie que pour l'amour d'elle, ils se rendirent Chevaliers errants' ('The planets are the wandering stars. Whereas the planets travel through the Zodiac, Pythagoras etc. were so in love with magic that they made themselves Knights errant'). All this also has Masonic overtones. There are indications in the vignettes in Gherardi's *Théâtre* that there is some connection with Freemasonry within the troupe and its plays (see overleaf).

Vingt-Sixiéme Ordre

The architecture of this *ordre* is discussed on p. 96.

La Convalescente

Probably a reference to Couperin's health, which was failing, as he admitted in the preface to *Book IV*.

Gavote

Clearly based on a vaudeville. The tune moves from part to part.

La Sophie

A whirling dervish or *sofi* (not a reference to a girl's name; see p. 96). One of the plays in Gherardi's collection was *Mezzetin en Grand Sofi* by Montchenay.[125] Bars 28–34 may portray the curious grunts dervishes make as they whirl.

L'Epineuse

Maria Teresa d'Orsi, the Spinette of Gherardi's troupe, the King's Comédiens Italiens. She was the sister-in-law of Mezzetin, Angelo Costantini (see *L'Angelique, Fifth Ordre*). Little is known about her but she made her début in 1697 in *Spinette lutin amoureux*, the last play done by Gherardi's troupe. She took several parts and received great acclaim and the title of universal actress.[126] The play

125. Montchenay, *Mezzetin en Grand Sofi*, in Gherardi, *Théâtre italien*, II.
126. Campardon, *Troupe Italienne*, p. 143.

Frontispiece of Gherardi, *Théâtre italien*, Vol. IV, Paris, 1700:
engraving by B. Audran after François Verdier

This shows the Masonic symbols of ladder and serpent

was revived in 1722 under the title *Le Lutin amoureux*. Like *L'Arlequine* (*Twenty-third Ordre*), another sadly nostalgic piece.

La Pantomime

A famous scene in which Scaramouche plays his guitar while waiting for his master to arrive. Pasquariel comes up noiselessly behind him and begins to beat time on his shoulders, which scares Scaramouche stiff. Couperin instructs that his *Pantomime* is to be played *d'une grande precision*. Gherardi writes of the celebrated pantomime of Scaramouche, Tiberio Fiorilli:

> C'est icy où cet Incomparable Scaramouche, qui a esté l'ornament du Théâtre, & le modele des plus Illustres Comediens de son temps, qui avoient appris de luy cet Art si difficile, & si necessaire aux personnes de leur caractere, de remuer les passions, & de les sçavoir bien peindre sur le visage; c'est icy, dis-je, où il faisoit pâmer de rire pendant un gros quart d'heure, dans une Scene d'épouvantes, où il ne proferoit pas un seul mot. Il faut convenir aussi, que cet excellent Acteur possedoit à un si haut degré de perfection ce merveilleux talent, qu'il touchoit plus de cœurs par les seules simplicitez d'une pure nature, que n'en touchent d'ordinaire les Orateurs les plus habiles par les charmes de la Rhetorique la plus persuasive.[127]

(It is this scene of the incomparable Scaramouche, the ornament of the stage and example to all the famous actors of his time, who had learnt from him the difficult and necessary art of simulating all the passions, and expressing them solely through the play of the features. It was in this pantomime of terror, indeed, that he made his audience rock with laughter for a good quarter of an hour, without once opening his mouth to speak. He possessed this marvellous talent to such a remarkable degree that he could, by the simplicity of pure nature alone, touch hearts more effectively than the most expert orators using the charms of the most persuasive rhetoric.)

127. Dufresny, *L'Avocat pour et contre*, in Gherardi, *Théâtre italien*, I, p. 377.

Vingt-Septiéme Ordre

L'Exquise, Allemande

The last *ordre* of all is a summary of all Couperin had been doing in his *Pièces de Clavecin*. *L'Exquise* is reminiscent of *La Couperin* of the *Twenty-first Ordre*. Furetière explains that *exquise* was used in the sense: 'Tout ce livre est plein de pensées exquises, expériences exquises, sentiments exquises' ('All this book is full of exquisite thoughts, exquisite experiences, exquisite sentiments').

Les Pavots

Poppies were a sleeping drug and Couperin was all too aware, as he said in his preface to *Book IV*, which was published in 1730, three years before he died, that it would be his last. The piece is reminiscent of the *sommeils* of Lully.

Les Chinois

A play by Regnard and Dufresny (see p. 64 and *Le Gaillard-Boiteux*, *Eighteenth Ordre*). In this play the French Isabelle manages, after certain obstacles have been removed, to marry her Italian lover Octave. This would be a subject in accordance with Couperin's desire, manifested in his chamber music, for *les goûts réunis*. The play opens on Mount Parnassus with Apollo and the Muses, and on the summit stands Pegasus (a symbol of literature) portrayed as a winged ass (see *La Conti*, *Sixteenth Ordre*). His braying keeps interrupting the conversation, and when Apollo asks Thalia, the muse of comedy, why the authors have not fed Pegasus, she tells him that: 'Les pauvres Diables ont bien de la peine à se nourrir eux-mesmes. Voyez-vous? Dans le temps où nous sommes, on n'engraisse guères à mâcher du Laurier'[128] ('The

128. Regnard and Dufresny, *Les Chinois*, in Gherardi, *Théâtre italien*, IV, p. 214.

poor devils can scarcely feed themselves. These days one can hardly get fat on chewing laurels'). This is very likely a reference to the fact that Couperin felt that he had not received enough money, or enough recognition, or both, in other words that all his exquisite compositions had not been sufficiently appreciated. That he had a slight chip on his shoulder is, possibly, revealed in his prefaces, and like most people of whom this is true, it was probably, to some extent, his own fault. Light is thrown on this by the son of the composer Claude Daquin, who was a pupil of one of Couperin's rivals, Marchand. He says that:

> These two men shared the affection of the public in their time and fought between themselves for first place. Marchand possessed rapidity of execution, a lively and sustained genius and a style of composing that only he could do. Couperin, less brilliant, less even, less favoured by nature, had more art, and according to several alleged connoisseurs was more profound. Sometimes, they say, he raised himself above his rival, but Marchand for two defeats gained twenty victories. He had no other epithet but *Le Grand*. He was a man of genius, work and reflection formed the other.[129]

Even when Daquin's evident prejudice in favour of his teacher is taken into account, this is one of the most revealing pieces of evidence there is on Couperin. Who nowadays is familiar with Matho, Mouret or de Blamont, composers who could turn out a *divertissement* in the night? Couperin had to watch their success, even possibly to sit at the harpsichord and be directed by them, when he knew he could have written better music himself. But this was not the point. People wanted things quickly. The poet

---

129. Daquin de Château Lyon, quoted in Bouvet, *Les Couperin*, p. 54. For interesting light on Couperin's character see Davitt Moroney, 'Couperin et les Contradicteurs: la révision de *L'Art de toucher le Clavecin*'.

Destouches wrote of Mouret, who was the Duchesse Du Maine's Surintendant de la Musique:

> A mesure que je composais les vers, feu Mr. Mouret les mettait en musique avec une facilité merveilleuse; en sorte que le Poète et le Musicien semblaient se disputer à qui aurait le plus tôt fini sa tâche.[130]

> (As I wrote the verses the late Mr. Mouret set them to music with a marvellous facility; so that the poet and the musician seemed in competition over who would finish the job soonest.)

As we know, Couperin himself said that he would rather be moved than astonished, but that was certainly not true of those who wanted entertainments.

The stage directions for the scene from *Les Chinois* say: 'A ridiculous ensemble of comic instruments is heard.' The second part of Couperin's *Les Chinois* is, like many of the pieces in *Book I*, awkward on the harpsichord, so probably it is yet another arrangement and may have started life as incidental music for the play. If, as Derek Connon suggests (see p. 70), this piece was originally the overture to *Les Chinois* and was intended to parody the portentous music of the opera, it is one of countless operatic parodies to be found in Gherardi's *Théâtre*.

Saillie

This word has many meanings. As well as a joke or a jump, it means a reproach, and it seems that Couperin is reproaching the public for not understanding his music. Furetière: 'Il se dit aussi de certains traits d'esprit brillants et surprenants qui semblent eschapper dans un Ouvrage d'éloquence, de poesie, dans la conversation' ('It is used also of certain brilliant and surprising shafts of

---

130. Viollier, *Jean-Joseph Mouret le musicien des grâces*, p. 216.

wit that seem to arise spontaneously in a work of eloquence, of poetry, in conversation'). In one of the most beautiful speeches from *Les Chinois*, Apollo reproaches someone who fails to understand the comic theatre, by saying:

> La Comédie forme l'esprit, élève le cœur, ennoblit les sentimens, c'est le miroir de la vie humaine qui fait voir le vice dans toute son horreur, & represente la vertu avec tout son éclat. Le Théâtre est l'Ecole de la politesse, le Rendez-vous des beaux esprits.[131]

> (Comedy forms the spirit, elevates the heart, ennobles the sentiments; it is the mirror of human life that shows vice in all its horror and virtue in all its magnificence. The theatre is the school of *politesse*, the rendez-vous of fine spirits.)

The implied obscenities of this scene, pointed out by Derek Connon (see pp. 68–9), are elevated by the nobility of Apollo's speeches onto a universal plane. Perhaps it was the contrasts in so many of the plays done by Gherardi's troupe that appealed to Couperin, and certainly the two halves of this final piece illustrate this dramatically. The first half is seriously contrapuntal, conversational, eloquent, poetic and very French, whilst the opening of the second brings us abruptly down to earth and is very Italian. It probably refers to the energetic ballet of acrobatic tricks, which would doubtless have been none too polite, in *Les Chinois*, described in the stage directions:

> On joue un air de violon sur lequel Pasquariel accompagné de quatre Sauteurs fait un Ballet de postures.[132]

> (An air is played on the violin, upon which Pasquariel accompanied by four tumblers does a ballet of acrobatic tricks.)

131. Regnard and Dufresny, *Les Chinois*, in Gherardi, *Théâtre italien*, IV, p. 219.
132. Regnard and Dufresny, *Les Chinois*, p. 250.

This part of the piece is certainly more grateful on the violin than on the harpsichord. It is surely the 'fine spirits' referred to by Apollo that Couperin speaks of in his preface to *Book III*, when he says his pieces 'will never make much of an impression on people of real discernment if all that I have indicated is not observed to the letter'. The scene in *Les Chinois* continues with Pierrot, dressed as a small girl, bewailing the fact that her mother will not allow her to go to the comedy because of the rude words. Apollo says that he can't think which words shock her mother:

> Pour moy, je n'y vois que des mots tout pleins de sel, qui à la verité sont quelquefois à double entente: mais toutes les plus belles pensées du monde ont deux faces, tant pis pour ceux qui ne les prennent que du mauvais côté; c'est une vraye marque de leur esprit corrompu & vicieux.

> (I find them full of salt, and although in truth they sometimes have a double meaning, all the most beautiful thoughts in the world have two sides, so much the worse for those who can only see the bad; it is a mark of their corrupted and vicious spirits.)

Those words might have come from Couperin himself. In this elusive final *ordre* it seems almost as though he is speaking to himself as he remembers the theatre that perhaps formed the model for his own 'mirror of human life', his *Pièces de Clavecin*.

JC

Bibliography

Antoine, Michel, 'Autour de François Couperin', *Revue de Musicologie*, 31 (1952), pp. 122–3

Aymon, Jean, François Gacon, Abbé de Margon and Abbé Desfontaines, *Mémoires pour servir à l'histoire de la Calotte* (Basle: 1725)

Bacilly, Bénigne de, *A Commentary upon the Art of Proper Singing, 1668*, trans. and ed. Austin B. Caswell (New York: Institute of Medieval Music, 1968)

Baecque, Antoine de, 'Les éclats du rire: le Régiment de la calotte, ou les stratégies aristocratiques de la gaieté française (1702–1752)', in *Annales, Histoire, Sciences Sociales*, 52 (1997), pp. 477–511

Baillet, Adrien, *La Vie de Monsieur Descartes* (Paris: Horthemels, 1691)

Ballard, Christophe, *Tendresses bachiques* (Paris: Mont-Parnasse, 1712)

Barthélemy, Maurice, 'Chaulieu à Châtenay', in *La Duchesse du Maine (1676–1753): une Mécène à la Croisée des Arts et des Siècles*, ed. Manuel Couvreur, Catherine Cessac and Fabrice Preyat (Brussels: Éditions de l'Université de Bruxelles, 2003), pp. 202–4

Baumgarten, J., *La France qui rit* (Cassel: Kay, 1880)

Baumont, Olivier, 'L'Ordre chez François Couperin', in *François Couperin; nouveaux regards*, ed. Huguette Dreyfus and Orhan Memed, Les Rencontres de Villecroze, 3 (Paris: Klincksieck, 1998), pp. 27–41

Beaussant, Philippe, *François Couperin*, trans. Alexandra Land (Portland, Oregon: Amadeus, 1990)

Blanc, André, *F. C. Dancourt (1661–1725). La Comédie française à l'heure du Soleil couchant*, Études littéraires françaises, 29 (Tübingen: Gunter Narr Verlag, and Paris: Place, 1984)

Bois-Jourdain, de, *Mélanges*, 3 vols (Paris: Chèvre et Chanson, 1807)

Bouvet, Charles, *Les Couperin* (Hildesheim and New York: Olms, 1977)

Braun, Lucinde, 'À la recherche de François Couperin', *Revue de Musicologie*, 95 (2009), pp. 37–64

Brossard, Sébastien de, *Dictionnaire de musique* (Paris: Ballard, 1703)

Cailleaux, Jean, 'Decorations by Watteau for the hôtel de Nointel', *Burlington Magazine* 103 (March 1961), No. 696, Supplement, pp. i–v

Calame, Alexandre, *Regnard, sa vie et son œuvre* (Paris: Presses Universitaires de France, 1960)

Campardon, Émile, *L'Académie Royale au XVIIIe siècle*, 2 vols (Paris: Berger-Levrault, 1884)

    Les Comédiens du Roi de la Troupe Française (Paris: Champion, 1879)

    Les Comédiens du Roi de la Troupe Italienne, 2 vols (Paris: Berger-Levrault, 1880)

Cessac, Catherine, 'La duchesse du Maine et la musique', in *La Duchesse du Maine (1676–1753): une Mécène à la Croisée des Arts et des Siècles*, ed. Manuel Couvreur, Catherine Cessac and Fabrice Preyat (Brussels: Éditions de l'Université de Bruxelles, 2003), pp. 97–107

    'Un portrait musical de la duchesse du Maine (1676–1753)', Programmes de concert: Versailles, 23 et 28 novembre 2003 (Versailles: Centre de Musique Baroque de Versailles, 2003), <http://philidor.cmbv.fr /jlbweb/jlbWeb?html=cmbv/BurAff&path=/biblio/bur/00/41/41.pdf&ext =pdf> [accessed December 2009]

Chung, David, 'Patronage and the development of French harpsichord music during Louis XIV's reign', in *Proceedings of the International Conference in Musicology, Early Music: Context and Ideas II*, Jagiellonian University, Krakow, Poland, September 2008, available at <http://www.muzykologia.uj.edu.pl/conference/>, pp. 100–118

Citron, Pierre, *Couperin* (Paris: Seuil, 1956)

Clark, Jane, 'Lord Burlington is here', in *Lord Burlington: Architecture, Art and Life*, ed. Toby Barnard and Jane Clark (London: Hambledon, 1995), pp. 251–310

Cohen, Albert, '"Un cabinet de musique" – the library of an eighteenth-century musician', in *Notes*, 59 (2002), pp. 20–37

Connon, Derek F., *Identity and Transformation in the Plays of Alexis Piron* (London: Legenda, 2007)

'Music in the Parisian Fair theatres: medium or message', in *Journal for Eighteenth-Century Studies*, 31 (2008), pp. 119–35

Connon, Derek F., and George Evans (eds), *Anthologie de pièces du 'Théâtre de la Foire'* (Egham: Runnymede, 1996)

Corp, Edward, 'Les courtisans français à la cour d'Angleterre à Saint-Germain-en-Laye', in *Cahiers de Saint Simon*, 28 (2000), pp. 49–66

'The exiled court of James II and James III: a centre of Italian music in France, 1689–1712', in *Journal of the Royal Musical Association*, 120 (1995), pp. 216–31

'François Couperin and the Stuart court at Saint-Germain-en-Laye, 1691–1712: a new interpretation', in *Early Music*, 28 (2000), pp. 445–53

'The Jacobite court at Saint-Germain-en-Laye', in *The Stuart Courts*, ed. Eveline Cruickshanks (London: Sutton, 2000), pp. 240–55

'The musical manuscripts of "Copiste Z"', in *Revue de musicologie*, 84 (1998), pp. 54–61

Covarrubias Horozco, Sebastián de, *Tesoro de la lengua castellana o española* (Madrid: Luis Sanchez, 1611)

Cowart, Georgia J., *The Triumph of Pleasure: Louis XIV and the Politics of Spectacle* (Chicago and London: University of Chicago Press, 2008)

'Watteau's *Pilgrimage to Cythera* and the subversive utopia of the opera-ballet', in *The Art Bulletin*, 83 (2001), pp. 461–78

Despois, Eugène, *Le Théâtre Français sous Louis XIV* (Paris: Hachette, 1874)

Dictionnaire de la langue française du seizième siècle (Paris: Champion, Didier, 1925–67)

Dufourcq, Norbert, and Marcelle Benoit, 'La vie musicale en Île de France sous la Régence: douze années à la Chapelle Royale de Musique d'après une correspondence inédite (1716–1728)', in *Revue de Musicologie*, 37 (1955), pp. 3–29, 148–85

Dufresny, Charles, *Les Amusements sérieux et comiques*, ed. Jean Vic (Paris: Bossard, 1921)

Du Noyer, Anne-Marguerite, *Lettres historiques et galantes*, 8 vols (Paris: Séguin, 1790)

Duranton, Henri, 'La très joyeuse et très véridique histoire du Regiment de la Calotte', in *Dix-Huitième Siècle*, 33 (2001), pp. 399–417

Fader, Don, 'The "Cabale du Dauphin", Campra, and Italian comedy: the courtly politics of French musical patronage around 1700', in *Music and Letters*, 86 (2005), pp. 380–413

Fleming, John, *Robert Adam and his Circle* (London: John Murray, 1962)

Franklin, Alfred, *La Vie privée d'autrefois*, 27 vols (Paris: Plon, Norrit, 1887–1902)

Fuller, David, 'Of portraits, "Sapho" and Couperin: titles and characters in French instrumental music of the High Baroque', in *Music and Letters*, 78 (1997), pp. 149–74

'Portraits and characters in instrumental music of seventeenth- and eighteenth-century France', in *Early Keyboard Journal*, 8 (1990), pp. 33–59

Furetière, Antoine, *Dictionnaire universel*, 3 vols (The Hague and Rotterdam: Arnout et Reinier Leers, 1960)

Garden, Greer, 'Un canon à cinq inédit de Couperin', *Bulletin de l'Atelier d'Études sur la Musique Française des XVIIe & XVIIIe Siècles*, 10 (2001–2002), pp. 16–17

Gherardi, Evaristo, ed., *Le Théâtre italien; ou, le Recueil général de toutes les comédies et scènes françoises jouées par les comédiens du roy, pendant tout le temps qu'ils ont été au service*, 6 vols (Paris: Cusson et Wiite, 1700)

Girdlestone, Cuthbert, *Jean-Philippe Rameau* (London: Cassell, 1957)

Glotz, Marguerite, and Madeleine Maire, *Salons du XVIIIe siècle* (Paris: Nouvelles Éditions Latines, 1949)

Griffiths, Bruce, 'Sunset: from *commedia dell'arte* to *comédie italienne*', in *Studies in the 'Commedia dell'arte'*, ed. D. George and C. Gossip (Cardiff: University of Wales Press, 1993), pp. 91–105

Grout, Donald Jay, 'The Music of the Italian Theatre at Paris, 1682–97', in *Journal of the American Musicological Society* (1941), pp. 158–70

Guyot, Joseph, *Regnard à Grillon* (Paris: Picard, 1907)

Histoire et recueil des Lazzis, ed. Judith Curtis and David Trott, Studies on Voltaire and the Eighteenth Century, 338 (Oxford: Voltaire Foundation, 1996)

Holman, Peter, 'An orchestral suite by François Couperin?', *Early Music*, 14 (1986), pp. 71–6

Howarth, William D., *et al.* (eds), *French Theatre in the Neo-Classical Era, 1550–1789* (Cambridge, New York, Melbourne: Cambridge University Press, 1997)

Isherwood, Robert M., *Farce and Fantasy: Popular Entertainment in Eighteenth-Century Paris* (Oxford: Oxford University Press, 1986)

Jullien, Adolphe, *Les Grandes Nuits de Sceaux, Le Théâtre de la Duchesse Du Maine* (Paris: Baur, 1876)

Landowska, Wanda, *Landowska on Music*, ed. Denise Restout (London: Secker and Warburg, 1965)

Le Brisoys Desnoiresterres, Gustave, *Cours galantes*, 4 vols (Paris: Dentu, 1862–5)

Ledbetter, David, '*Les goûts réunis* and the music of J. S. Bach', in *Basler Jahrbuch für Historische Musikpraxis*, 28 (2004), pp. 63–80

Le Laboureur, Louis, *Avantages de la langue françoise sur la langue latine* (Paris: F. Lambert, 1667)

Letters from Liselotte see Orléans, Duchesse d'

Levron, Jacques, *Daily Life at Versailles*, trans. Claire Engel (London: Allen and Unwin, 1968)

Lewis, W. H., *The Sunset of the Splendid Century* (London: Eyre and Spottiswoode, 1955)

Lindgren, Lowell, 'Parisian patronage of performers from the Royal Academy of Musick (1719–28)', *Music and Letters* 58 (1977), pp. 4–28

Maland, David, *Culture and Society in Seventeenth-Century France* (London: Batsford, 1970)

Maurel, André, *La Duchesse du Maine Reine de Sceaux* (Paris: Hachette, 1928)

Maurepas, *Recueil*, dit de Maurepas, *Pièces Libres, Chansons, Epigrammes*, 6 vols (Leyden: 1865)

Mellers, Wilfrid, *François Couperin and the French Classical Tradition* (London: Faber & Faber, 1987)

Mirimonde, A.-P. de, 'Les sujets musicaux chez Antoine Watteau', *Gazette des beaux arts* (1961), pp. 249–88

Mitford, Nancy, *The Sun King* (London: Sphere Books, 1969)

Mongrédien, Georges, *Daily Life in the French Theatre*, trans. Claire Engel (London: Allen and Unwin, 1969)

Montéclair, Michel Pignolet de, *Brunètes anciènes et modernes* (Paris: Boivin, n. d.)

Moroney, Davitt, 'Couperin et les Contradicteurs: la révision de *L'Art de toucher le Clavecin*', in *François Couperin; nouveaux regards*, ed. Huguette Dreyfus and Orhan Memed, Les Rencontres de Villecroze, 3 (Paris: Klincksieck, 1998), pp. 163–86

'The parodies of François Couperin's harpsichord pieces', in *'L'Esprit français' und die Musik Europas: Festschrift für Herbert Schneider*, ed. M. Biget-Mainfoy and Rainer Schmusch (Hildesheim: Olms, 2007), pp. 608–33

Naudon, Paul, *Freemasonry: A European Viewpoint*, trans. Joseph Tsang (Tunbridge Wells: Freestone Press, 1993)

Orléans, Duchesse d', *Letters from Liselotte, Élisabeth Charlotte, Princess Palatine and Duchess of Orléans*, trans. and ed. Maria Kroll (London: Gollancz, 1970)

Orléans, Duchesse d', *The Letters of Madame*, trans. and ed. Gertrude Scott Stevenson, 2 vols (London: Chapman and Dodd Arrowsmith, 1924–5)

Parfaict, Claude and François, *Histoire du Théâtre-Français depuis son origine jusqu'à présent*, 15 vols (Paris: Le Mercier et Saillant, 1734–49)

Mémoires pour servir à l'histoire des spectacles de la foire. Par un acteur forain, 2 vols (Paris: Briasson, 1743)

Petrie, Sir Charles, *The Duke of Berwick and his Son* (London: Eyre and Spottiswoode, 1951)

Piépape, General de, *A Princess of Strategy*, trans. J. Lewis May (London and New York: John Lane, 1911)

Plax, Julie Anne, *Watteau and the Cultural Politics of Eighteenth-Century France* (Cambridge: Cambridge University Press, 2000)

Pomey, Père François, in *Dictionnaire royal augmenté* (Lyon: Antoine Molin, 1671)

Replat, Jacques, *Voyage au long cours sur le Lac d'Annecy* (Annecy: Philippe, 1858)

Robinson, Philip, 'Les vaudevilles: un médium théâtral', in *Dix-huitième siècle*, 28 (1996), pp. 431–47

Rousseau, Jean-Jacques, *Dictionnaire de musique* (Paris: Veuve Duchesne, 1768)

Sadie, Stanley (ed.), *The New Grove Dictionary of Music & Musicians*, 20 vols (London: Macmillan, 1980)

Sadler, Graham, 'A philosophy lesson with François Couperin?', *Early Music*, 32 (2004), pp. 541–7

Saint Simon, Duc de, *Historical Memoirs of the Duc de Saint Simon*, ed. Lucy Norton, 3 vols (London: Hamish Hamilton, 1967–72)

Sawkins, Lionel, *A Thematic Catalogue of the Works of Michel-Richard de Lalande (1657–1726)* (Oxford: Oxford University Press, 2005)

Scott, Virginia, *The 'Commedia dell'Arte' in Paris, 1644–1697* (Charlottesville: University Press of Virginia, 1990)

Staal de Launay, Madame de, *Memoirs*, trans. Cora Hamilton Bell, 2 vols (London: Osgood and MacIlvane, 1892)

Titon Du Tillet, Évrard, *Le Parnasse françois* (Paris: 1734)

Tunley, David, *The Eighteenth-Century French Cantata* (London: Dennis Dobson, 1974)

   François Couperin and 'The Perfection of Music' (Aldershot: Ashgate, 2004)

Venard, Michèle, *La Foire entre en scène* (Paris: Librairie Théâtrale, 1985)

Verèb, Pascale, *Alexis Piron, poète (1689–1773); ou, la Difficile Condition d'auteur sous Louis XV*, Studies on Voltaire and the Eighteenth Century, 349 (Oxford: Voltaire Foundation, 1997)

Viollier, Renée, *Jean-Joseph Mouret le musicien des grâces, 1682–1738* (Paris: Floury, 1950; reprinted Geneva: Minkoff, 1976)

Index

Pages including illustrations are shown in *italic*.

INDEX